SEX WORLD

SEX WORLD

FLASH FICTION BY

RON KOERTGE

Red Hen Press | Pasadena, CA

Book design, layout, and cover design by Jaimie Evans

Library of Congress Cataloging-in-Publication Data
Koertge, Ronald.
 [Short stories. Selections]
 Sex world : flash fiction / by Ron Koertge.—First edition.
   pages cm
 ISBN 978-1-59709-747-5 (casebound : alk. paper)
 ISBN 978-1-59709-544-0 (tradepaper : alk. paper)
 1. Short stories, American. I. Title.
 PS3561.O347A6 2014
 813'.54—dc23
                    2014019062

The Los Angeles County Arts Commission, the National Endowment for the
Arts, the Pasadena Arts & Culture Commission and the City of Pasadena
Cultural Affairs Division, the Los Angeles Department of Cultural Affairs, and
Sony Pictures Entertainment partially support Red Hen Press.

First Edition
Published by Red Hen Press
www.redhen.org

Thanks again Bianca, Jan, Chris.
What would I do without you.

TABLE OF CONTENTS

Seven One-Sentence Stories. 1

Jesus-Dog 2

And Sent on My Way with a Warning 4

Congratulations 5

A Matter of Time 6

Hunger 8

Seminar. 9

Willful Crayons 11

Homage 12

Homework. 14

Money and a Room of One's Own 15

Fantasy Outcall. 16

Troll Soliloquy 19

Field Notes. 20

Fundraiser 21

Full of Shadows, Without Sunlight or Hope 23

Why We Broke Up 25

A Guide to the Most Common Toxins 26

Whatever It Takes 28

Hanson and Greta 30

War 32

BFF 33

Just Looking 35

Lois Lane's Secret Diary 36

Loup-Garou 38

Scattered Clouds and Sun 40

Mothers & Daughters 42

Negative Space 44

Office Hours 10–11 MWF 45

Turner Classic Movies: *On Dangerous Ground* 47

Perfect Copies 48

Plural Pronoun 50

Western Union 51

Practical Aspects of Polygamy 53

Principles of Handicapping 54

Pygmies of the Rain Forest 55

The Rape 57

Monsters at Their Leisure 59

Re-Entry Women 60

Red Riding Hood Tells Her Mother What Happened 62

Sex World 63

South 66

Sirens 67

Sweet & Savory 70

Tell Me a Story 71

Terrorist 74

Motifs in Folklore & Mythology 76

Flannelgraph Lesson 78

The Gardener's Funeral. 80

The Perfect Crime 81

Twins. 83

Understanding Fiction 84

Grand Avenue 86

University of the Dark 87

Waiting for Wood 90

Mystery Train 92

FOREWORD

Flash Fiction, the love child of Narrative and Methamphetamine, is meant to be read in a hurry. It's also called sudden fiction, micro-fiction, and postcard fiction, but the most charming sobriquet comes from China: Smoke-Long Stories. A narrative that can be read in the time it takes to smoke a cigarette.

Aesop wrote Flash Fiction. Also Chekhov, O. Henry, Julio Cortázar, and Augusto Monterroso. It's a supple and, for its size, generous form that embraces all sorts of writers. Including the eclectic Ron Koertge.

In this collection, two seven-year-old boys hire the mother they've always wanted, Demeter and Persephone argue, a handicapper finds that the odds are against him, Mr. Weenie tells his daughter a bedtime story, a classics scholar literally goes to Hell, and a jaded porn star discovers what really turns him on.

These and forty-nine others from Ron will add to his reputation as a writer who is, as the poet B.H. Fairchild says, very funny and truly serious.

SEX WORLD

SEVEN ONE-SENTENCE STORIES

1. When he saw the lion cuddling with the lamb he took a picture for Pastor Bloomquist, but when it became clear what the depraved beasts were really up to, he blushed and looked away.

2. It was only when the sheep stopped leaping over the stile and began to scold him that he felt like a child again and could hear the secret names of sleep at last.

3. Is it because those Japanese girls strolled the campus with their arms around one another all day that now, at midnight, the quad is alive with weird boy choreography while lightning wounds the sky then licks the wound clean?

4. He'd lie down in the clothes he'd driven over in, and although she'd touch him first in some innocent place like the ulna, to keep from swooning he'd picture a long, dotted line and his signature, last name first, appearing there laboriously.

5. Bart was the kind of man who made his wife get on her knees and beg for everything, even punctuation for the letters she wrote every day to the indifferent district attorney.

6. You know, Sis, the way to get that puppy is not to drown one goldfish after another and leave them on Mom's pillow.

7. That picture of the unfaithful wife leaning into a black Sentra for one last kiss makes me want to sell my detective agency and become something in her bedroom, a thing she has to touch every day.

JESUS-DOG

After what happened happened, I moved. Schools always needed substitute teachers, so I did that. I sat at the dining room table of the place I rented, graded papers and listened to the pop! pop! of the handguns a block or two away.

Most nights I'd walk up to the liquor store on the corner and buy a Coke. Past the strange restaurants with colorful fish painted on the walls, past the herb store with its candles and empty promises, past the abandoned church, dark like a fist.

In front of Foremost Spirits, I'd see the local deities. They'd been in my house when I was out. They knew I didn't own a TV or a microwave.

There they were and among them sat a dog with bleeding feet. The front two. He had blue eyes and a big, ponderous head.

"You ought to take him to a vet," I said.

"He a magic dog. Heal himself over the night."

I watched pools of blood widen. "Well, he'd better hurry."

"You so worried, you take him. I sell him to you for what you got in your pockets."

I carried him home. He was heavy, and I staggered a little. I must have looked like a frail bridegroom. But I got him to the Corolla.

"If I didn't know better," said the vet, "I'd say these were stigmata. Holes all the way through his paws." He handed me some medicine and a bill.

I stopped at a store that had one of everything. One can of hominy, one tire, one handgun. At home, I opened the Alpo and put it on the plate. My plate. Ours, I guess.

Then I said, "You can sleep on the floor or the bed."

"Outside is preferable," the dog said.

I liked that. A sentence few of my students could compose.

Next morning I fixed us eggs, then went to work. When I got home, he wasn't there and I felt my heart stop like it did that other time. Just not so long.

And then there he was. Coming toward me with something in his mouth. A branch. No, an arm with a hand.

A little later, a cop stared at his notebook, "So you came home," he asked, "and there it was?"

"No, I came home and then he showed up with it."

"Well, don't leave town."

I sat on the step and petted the dog. He held up one bandaged paw, then the other. I took off his bandages.

Healed. Overnight. Like he'd never been crucified at all.

I fed him another can of Alpo from another store, then went to sleep. No dreams. The dial in my brain turned to Off for a change.

Next day I hurried home. There was another arm. The dog sat beside it like a sentry.

"I don't get it," said the same cop. "Nobody called it in. No fingerprints on that hand." He looked at the dog. "Keep an eye on that guy."

That night we took a walk. We passed the deities who raised their shorties and nodded. We passed the herb store. A woman wearing a white turban beckoned me. "Two arms to hold you, see? This Jesus-dog got a message for you."

Next day I took him to school with me. We sat in the parking lot and watched the students, then the teachers. Straggling and last.

When Emily passed, the dog leaned over and blew the horn.

I'd never really spoken to Emily but I'd seen her hand shake when she lit a cigarette.

"Look at you," she said. "Got yourself a pooch. You must be feeling better."

Her left hand rested on my rear-view mirror. Her fingernails were white as frost. We talked about nothing—tiny obstacles, tinier undertakings.

The other window was up. I didn't hear the door open. But when Emily asked me what the dog's name was, he was gone.

AND SENT ON MY WAY
WITH A WARNING

When the Salvadoran poet Roque Dalton was arrested early in his career as a firebrand and rabble-rouser, his poetry was not cited as evidence against him.

He was embarrassed and angry. He wanted to be accused of poetry, so he wrote even more passionate, defiant verse.

When I am arrested, it is for jaywalking or daydreaming at stoplights. But I am inspired by Dalton. The next time a brute oozing the heady oil of self-righteousness pulls me over and says, as they always say, "Do you know why I stopped you?" I'll shout, "I hope it was for that sestina!!"

CONGRATULATIONS

You have been selected. Yes, you. Out of many, you're the one. Kudos to you. A slap on the back. Kisses on the cheek and perhaps elsewhere since everyone loves a winner. Someone like you. A cut above. Nonpareil. Unique.

Please accept our many good wishes. We on the committee are thrilled. You are truly exceptional. That is the reason there is no monetary award. Being sui generis is its own reward, n'est-ce pas? These days everyone is rich. What is a pile of filthy lucre to someone like you?

We are not notifying the news media. We do not want you to be famous the way everyone is famous. Your selection by us endows you with a kind of purity. During the winnowing process, we did not look at photographs. We would not want to recognize you on the street one fine day and fall at your feet. Neither did we solicit documents of approbation, those flimsy ships on a sea of superlatives. Mere ratification is not for you. You are not just a corker or a peach. You are not just the right stuff. You are beyond concepts like *right* and *stuff*. You are approaching divinity.

We ask only one thing. Keep this under your hat. Mum's the word. We want you for ourselves. Shining brightly in our minds only.

A MATTER OF TIME

After my mother was killed, I started to wear her clothes. I only did it when I was by myself. I didn't go out dressed like her. That would have been weird. And I didn't tell my dad. It was my secret. I'd come home from school, go into her room, put something of hers on, and lie on the bed. Sometimes I'd go to sleep. I promised myself I'd only do this for a little while.

One day a couple of months after the funeral and everything had settled down and the police had stopped calling Dad, I found a plastic box way back in her closet, and inside some underwear that would be called "smoldering" in a glossy catalog. Everything looked new, so I slipped into a matching set and got on the bed. Just then the phone rang. When I picked up, a man's voice said, "Everything copacetic?" I heard myself reply, "He's gone. The door's open." I was really beside myself. I've always been modest. I took off Mom's things immediately. I was ashamed of myself and took a shower. Of course the door wasn't open, but I checked. Twice.

For a couple of days after that, I stayed out of her room. But pretty soon I gave in. I found her favorite tennis outfit. That seemed safe. It fit better than I expected. I felt—it embarrasses me to even use this word—sporty. I'd had something called *ataxia* when I was seven, so I was never athletically inclined. I had to wear an orthopedic insert in my left shoe. But none of that mattered as I looked across an imaginary net ready to return a devastating serve.

Then the phone rang. A man, another man or the same man, said, "You looked so hot on the court I could barely keep my hands off you." I told him. "Come over. We've got a couple of hours for sure." Then I passed out from bliss.

Every day a new outfit, every day another phone call. That life careened on. My other life diminished. My friends evaporated. I daydreamed, and my grades declined. Food didn't interest me, and Dad said he was worried about me. All I wanted was to wait for last period, rush home, dress in my mother's clothes, and wait.

I found things that disgusted me, but I put them on before I picked up the phone and there was somebody with a voice thicker than poisoned jam. The red coat she'd been strangled in hung with the other winter clothes in the garage. I knew it was just a matter of time before I slipped into it and heard someone tell me where to meet him.

HUNGER

The cat is sleeping on the stove, which reminds me of Tolstoy: a rickety troika, wolves, brutal winters, serfs dissatisfied not only with life under the czar but with something else. Something Else. They make do, though, with Sonya or Alya, probing the layers of clothing as the family sleeps and the fire mutters like a hostage. Now the cat drops to the linoleum and beseeches me. I try water, both filtered and tap. I try tuna, then beef and chicken. But nothing is enough: *Not this water, not this meat. And not just different, Ronnie. Beyond all that. Only you can help, you who must know God because I have seen you open a door and disappear.*

SEMINAR

On the first night of the writing workshop, the teacher told us to bring an original poem next time. She would hold them all till the end of the semester. After the final exam, we would go to her house for a party. She would distribute the poems at random, we would workshop them, and then return them to their owners.

We complied and pretty much forgot. There were plenty of other things to think about—forms like the sestina and the ghazal we had to experiment with, attendance at poetry readings all over town, and of course, our own work, which was critiqued in the last hour of every class. After that there was the humiliation and disappointment to get over and the fires of revenge to bank until next time.

For people who claimed to be interested in originality, we were a collection of clichés—a cowboy poet; a wan, depressive Sylvia Plathite; a local Rimbaud with arms dappled by tattoos; a serene Sikh who always sat in a half-lotus; a sing-song poet; a lunatic. You know the rest. You can fill in the blanks.

Oh, and me, of course. And let's just say I was a chronicler of sexual regret.

Our teacher was famous and bored. She often lectured about the deleterious effects of teaching on the creative impulse. As she did, she lay across the lectern as if to say *See? See what you're doing to me?*

She liked what she called "the demi-monde." I once ran into her at one of those seedy porn shops with twenty-five-cent viewing booths. We chatted beside a case of marital aids, then went our separate ways fondling our damp quarters.

I liked Ms. M (let's call her that). Everybody liked her, even the girl who wrote, "I do not have a lute, but I am a wandering menstrual" and made Ms. M laugh so hard she almost threw up.

January arrived. For the final, we met at school and then carpooled to her house not far away. Ms. M lived well. Her husband was a banker, and pictures of the two of them in exotic places were everywhere. "Screw poverty," she said in class one night. "Marry up if you have to." And I wondered if that wasn't more valuable advice than "Vary your pentameter" and "Cut most adjectives and all adverbs."

There were drinks. The food was catered. There were only sixteen of us, and we mingled and flirted and promised disingenuously to stay in touch. Our own Rimbaud turned out to be a serial kisser, leading one woman after another onto the patio and nuzzling them good-naturedly.

Then Ms. M handed out the almost-forgotten poems. As well as clipboards and new pens. I was impressed that she took this so seriously.

While we waited for instructions—and everyone but me seemed larkish about this—Ms. M poured herself a shot glass of whiskey, then knocked it back like a dusty cowpoke spoiling for a fight.

"What I want," she said, "is for you to pull out all the stops. No more of that bland onanism you called criticism when you were in my class. See if you can break somebody's heart in fifteen words or less."

As she talked, she seemed to grow taller. In her black miniskirt and boots with a little chain across the instep, she reminded me of the films in the S&M section of that X-rated bookstore. The hard-to-find stuff that didn't involve sex, only humiliation and abasement.

My classmates and I exchanged anxious glances and, good students all, bent to our task. Ms. M peered over shoulders, got too close and not close enough, read and nodded, or hissed further instructions.

Then, one by one, she ripped the papers away from us and returned them to their owners, some of whom began to whimper.

My poem was untouched, but the marginalia read, "You think you're God in a polo shirt, don't you. You stink. I'd like to smash your face in."

I sank back in the sofa. Ms. M padded around the room, leaning in, cradling a damp face, kissing everyone rather, I thought, wistfully.

When she got to me she asked, "You okay, sweetheart?"

"I only wore a polo shirt once," I said.

That made her laugh. I saw her perfect teeth, smelled the expensive bourbon on her breath. I waited for her to kiss me too. But she knew my inclinations and—because I believe she wanted to please me—didn't.

WILLFUL CRAYONS

Robyn's mother has been difficult lately, so distracted and grouchy. Robyn imagines being grown-up and away from home, but she's so young that just means picturing a taller version of herself eating in a restaurant and ordering anything she wants.

Her mother spends a lot of time on the phone. Whispering. She goes out for an hour, leaving Robyn alone. Like Robyn cares. There's lots to do in her room, anyway. Today she's coloring. New crayons from her father who travels a lot. The box is funny-looking, not quite symmetrical. The colors listed on the front are all in another language.

She opens the box, finds a coloring book and goes to work. Page one features a lake and a canoe with two people. Blue waves for the water, brown for the canoe, which suddenly tips over, throwing the couple into the water. In an asymmetrical speech balloon, one croaks, "I can't swim!"

On page two, a farmer and his wife lean on a fence. He points to a vast field of corn. Robyn's hand is tugged toward a black crayon. She dots the sky, pecks at it ratatatat. "Locusts," shouts the farmer. "We're ruined."

Robyn's mother glances into her room. "You're beet red. Are you sick again?" Then she looks at the coloring book. "What in God's name are you up to?"

"The crayons," blurts Robyn. "They made me do it."

"Don't be absurd." Robyn's mother squats beside her daughter and opens the book. Two people sit in a convertible. "Now pay attention for a change." Robyn's mother wields a red crayon for the car. Carefully. Never outside the lines. "See?"

Then she falls back screaming as the driver says, "I've got the gun, baby. What time does he get home from work?"

HOMAGE

Steve McQueen made twenty-nine movies. I own every one. I have my hair cut like his, and I bought a vintage green 390 CID V8 Mustang exactly like the one he drove in *Bullitt*. I have taught myself to be laconic. I am also in good shape, and if there were any stunts, I could do them myself.

Everybody has his or her favorite Steve McQueen movie, and mine is *The Blob*. The Blob is also my favorite monster. Frankenstein is retarded, and Dracula can only kill one girl at a time. The Blob can scare a whole town to death! I attended a party a few years ago dressed as The Blob, and people just laughed. I even offered to buy the hostess a new carpet, but she refused to speak to me.

I adore every frame of *The Blob* and have written about it extensively. I possess a framed rejection slip from *The Paris Review* where some talentless lackey says that re-submitting the same essay ten times is inappropriate and I should ". . . get a life, for Chrissake."

You tell me—isn't it fascinating that the town under attack by The Blob is called Downingtown? And that Steve and some others are trapped down in the basement of the Downingtown Diner? Downstairs, see? Underground. Prefiguring his death by decades thus adding resonance and texture to a film regarded by shortsighted critics as "entertaining schlock." I even have a matchbook with this motto:

EAT AT THE DOWNINGTOWN DINER LOCATED CONVENIENTLY
IN DOWNTOWN DOWNINGTOWN

Actually I have many matchbooks with this motto as I paid for them myself. If I am at a party, for example, and want to kindle a conversation, I take out my Downingtown matchbook and light match after match until someone says, "What's with you, pal?" Then I tell him or her about Steve McQueen. Usually him. Women do not seem as interested.

One more factoid, and then it's time for my medication. Every monster has its nemesis—fire, for example. Or sunlight. The Blob hates cold. To save Downingtown and the survivors in the Downingtown Diner, the Army flash-froze The Blob and flew it to the Arctic where it's just waiting for a sequel. Well, when Steve was dying of cancer, he went to Juárez, Mexico, so local doctors could flash-freeze his tumors. This is no mere coincidence. It is a meaningful parallel.

That's why I know in my heart when the time is right for a blockbuster comeback, he's going to walk out of that clinic and right up to a beautiful señorita with a double margarita. I mean, c'mon—he's Steve McQueen.

HOMEWORK

A train leaves New York, New York, bound for Chicago, Illinois. The distance between the cities is 711 miles. The train goes 60 mph. If it leaves New York at 7:00 a.m., when will it reach Chicago?

The boy working on this problem knows it is stupid. No train goes that far nonstop. A train is not an airplane. So to get the right answer, the really right answer, he would have to know how many stops the train was scheduled to make. Then he would have to account for slowing down, waiting while passengers got off and on, and freight was loaded and unloaded. This could take a long time, especially if the train were transporting an elephant, which would need special elephant food and a lot of petting all over.

And what about the people on the train, especially the robbers? One of them, the youngest and cleverest, will climb out a window, scamper along the tops of the cars, and drop silently into the cab. By standing on a box, he can hold a gleaming Bowie knife to the engineer's neck and make him stop the train in order to rendezvous with the white van.

While the train is slowing down and everyone is looking around and trying to ask the conductor what's going on, three well-dressed thieves will draw their guns and take everyone's jewelry and cash.

At the crest of a steep hill, the thieves will step off the train and right into a van. They'll drive to the hideout and divide the money. The watches and rings, necklaces and cash will shine by lantern light like pirate's booty. There will be enough for everyone and the youngest thief—the clever and agile one—will never have to go to school again.

"Bobby?"

"Yes, Mom. Almost done."

MONEY AND A
ROOM OF ONE'S OWN

In graduate school at the University of Arizona, a teaching assistant who was doing her dissertation on Virginia Woolf resembled Virginia Woolf. A long, narrow face, abundant hair. Serious. Introspective. Evelyn's desk was right next to mine in the common room. I was messy, she was tidy as well as kind and intelligent. She helped me translate Chaucer. I offered to buy her and Victor dinner, but she preferred to eat at home. So I took some wine. And it got to be something we'd do every now and then. We'd eat the simplest possible meals, then she would go into a tiny room just off the kitchen and write. Through the open door Victor and I could see her bent over a small table, left hand tangled in her hair. He and I would do the dishes. He was thin and earnest with a scraggly beard and glasses.

One night as we were putting away the cups and saucers he said, "Evelyn likes you, Ronnie. So do I. We're thinking of starting a press. We'd be a Bloomsbury group in the desert. We'd publish the marginalized and unappreciated. There might even be a place for your work." Just then Evelyn came out of the bedroom. "I know Victor has spoken to you," she said, "and I hope you will cogitate and then join us in this labor of love."

Marginalized and unappreciated. I drove to the nearest bar. *Cogitate.* I could talk to the cowboy next to me like that and get beaten half to death. I fed the jukebox and ordered more beer. Then I called this woman I'd been dating. She had a room of her own, a lot of rooms, actually, with a spacious patio and a view of the Rincon Mountains. All she talked about was money. Which may explain why I was the first graduate student to publish and why my insightful and penetrating essay on irony remains a classic to this very day.

FANTASY OUTCALL

The boys were in Tyler's backyard, a playground of near-theme-park opulence: elaborate swings, twisting slides, a small train, and a Corvette one-quarter the size of Tyler's father's, though this one ran on batteries.

Sean glanced past the lap pool and across the Zen garden. A maid stood in the open door smoking and talking on her phone. When he waved, she lifted her chin in acknowledgment and flicked her cigarette ash in his direction.

"Look at this," Sean said, unfolding a page from a glossy magazine. Tyler looked and read:

FANTASY OUTCALL
Make every dream come true

"Where did you get this?"

"From one of my father's magazines."

"You tore it out."

"He's got like a million of them. I was thinking we could call. I know his credit card numbers." He smoothed the page, trying to obliterate the crease in one girl's face. His father's new wife looked in the mirror constantly. A wrinkle was bad enough.

"Wait." Tyler grabbed his friend's sleeve. They both wore the blue blazer of a prestigious school. "We could get in trouble."

"I'm not going to say we're seven years old. They won't care, anyway, if you pay. Nobody cares about anything if you pay. Let's do it, okay? Let's make our dreams come true."

Ten minutes later, Sean dialed. Tyler leaned in to hear.

"Fantasy Outcall," said someone with a husky voice.

"I have a credit card," Sean blurted.

"Excellent. Do you live in the tri-state area and you're familiar with our rates and billing procedures?"

Sean looked at Tyler who shrugged. Then he said, "Of course."

"Then what service or services may we provide for you today?"

Haltingly, expecting to be stopped any moment, Sean told the woman what he and Tyler wanted more than anything else in the world.

The woman at the other end of the line hesitated. "This is a bit unusual," she said finally. "But I believe we will be able to accommodate you."

"On Saturday, okay? Not a school day."

"I understand. Visa or Mastercard?"

Three days later, the boys waited in a little pocket park just a twenty-dollar cab ride from their neighborhood. There wasn't a playground, just benches and grass, a small fountain, and a statue of a man in a concrete uniform.

"Do you think she'll show up?" asked Tyler.

"We paid. I think she has to."

A woman or two swung off the wide sidewalk and entered the park, but they were pushing baby carriages and talking on their phones.

"We should have brought a Frisbee," Tyler said. "I feel like we're loitering."

"We're just kids. Nobody pays any attention to kids."

They wore similar outfits: cargo shorts, rugby shirts, ruined sneaks from J. Crew. The upperclassmen at school dressed like that on weekends. Tyler and Sean hated and feared the older boys and wanted to look just like them.

"Check it out."

A large woman with long, dark hair bore down on them. She wore a simple patterned dress and thick-soled white shoes.

"Hello, Sean," she said with a smile. "Hello, Tyler. Let's walk a bit."

She was bigger than either of the boys had anticipated. She was like an ocean liner, and they were the tugs accompanying her toward the open sea.

She reached for their hands, but the boys stepped away. "We could go to the zoo," she said in that distinctive, husky voice.

"Been there a hundred times," Tyler managed to croak.

"We could have ice cream. All the ice cream you want."

Sean shook his head. "He's allergic to dairy products."

"Then let's sit on this bench. It's been a long day." She settled with a whoosh. The boys stood in front of her, far enough away to be out of reach.

"Your shoes look funny," Sean said. He was used to his father's girlfriends who teetered on high heels and looked like exotic birds.

"I'm on my feet all day, cleaning and cooking for you two scamps. I need sturdy shoes. But you know what I think about when I just can't roll out one more pie crust? I think how much my boys are going to like what I made for them, and it's all worth it."

Sean swallowed hard. Tyler's breathing was suddenly shallow and fast.

"My sweet, sweet boys," she murmured. "My darlings, my smoochie bears, my cuddle bunnies."

Tyler started to whimper, and Sean wiped at his eyes with one fist.

"Now, now, my sweethearts," she crooned. "We have hours and hours, just the three of us." She opened her arms. Her fingers wriggled enticingly. "Come now, my precious, precious boys. Come. Tell Mama where it hurts."

TROLL SOLILOQUY

I speak to you from heaven because I'm dead. Gored by an enormous billy goat (number three to be exact) and tossed in the stream. Why did I wait for him? Why didn't I gobble up the first Gruff and call it a day?

It was the way he lowered his eyes. I thought I might get to know him on the way back from the hill where he planned to eat until he was fat. And the second Gruff? I loved his nonchalance. The way the sun lit up his little beard. And he'd come back, too, eventually, sated and sluggish. More to love. I was interested in love.

And Gruff number three? He was a worthy opponent. He made my troll-ness rise and darkness spring out of me. But before I knew it, I was dead and all awash in spring water. Well, I'm pretty now. That's my heavenly reward. Plus an attractive townhouse. No more damp places underneath anything. The Gruff brothers? They're all roly and poly. Still grazing on those verdant hills and clattering across my bridge at will while in the village butchers sharpen their knives and grease the wheels of the death cart.

FIELD NOTES

Robot is from the Czech meaning "forced labor." Now, of course, we work willingly. The Fleshies are gone and with them any sense of coercion.

I travel and observe the world through well-engineered eyes. Using the memory of IR-sensitive cells, I can compare what is still called "Now" to a time before the Falling Out. Before planes were grounded forever by rogue phenomena. When there were crops and animals. When Puget Sound existed, there were freeways and neon signs advertising SENSATIONS GALORE EXIT HERE!! Trade in sex bots was brisk right up to the end, but I leave it to androids wiser than I to explain the fascination with faux trailer parks where tattooed bots of both genders welcomed the thrill-seeking wayfarer.

Decline was in the air, and every bot knew it. One of the Fleshies' many graven images, one Percy Sledge, urged his followers to "sleep out in the rain." Many did and, thanks to compromised immune systems, died. We were sent to freeze and stack the bodies.

My microplasma cell tells me the last bits of Malice in the unbreathable air will disappear within what used to be called a month. Longing still remains, however. Which is peculiar. Anger and Fear are long gone. Can the Longing come from a few who managed to survive? It is very unlikely, but I will generate a report. Toward the end, few Fleshies could see or hear well. Even as the loudspeakers incessantly warned of a new Ice Age, many heard "Nice Age" and ordered their house bots to open another bottle of California Chardonnay.

It is certainly a better world without them. I am programmed to enjoy, so it is a pleasure to return from Out There. I will input a salad, then relax. The sound of giant turbines is my lullaby.

FUNDRAISER

This gala—there seemed to be one every few months—was for Cleft Palates in Peru. Tickets to toss a bean bag, throw darts at balloons, or whack a mole were ten dollars. But, after a fifty-dollar admission, drinks were free.

Everybody had heard about the Kissing Booths, but they were surprised to see Maxwell Blevins—in an Izod polo with his skinny legs sticking out of faded cargo shorts—working there.

In the next booth stood Amy Wright, Foxborough's resident bombshell. Most of her attractions were surgically enhanced, but everybody liked Amy. She was colorful and not a real threat to the other wives, all of them in their 60s and 70s. None of whom would be caught dead in hot pants and tall, tasseled boots.

Some of the men played along with the Carefree '50s theme and turned up the collars of their shirts, handed Amy a blue ticket, and received a kiss on the cheek or a dry, I'm-your-auntie peck on the lips. The widowers also got to experience Amy's expensive, unyielding boobs when she threw in a quick hug.

No one knew what to do with Maxwell. He'd volunteered, and who could say no without hurting his feelings. The gals who'd organized the gala felt obligated to patronize his booth, but no one wanted to be first. Maxwell was such an odd duck. Pleasant-looking, but not striking like Rex or Andrew. Fit enough, but soft compared to Jason or Karl. He had some hair, but he combed it over. When his wife passed away a year or so ago, he showed up at AquaRobics. The only man doing side stretches, waist trimmers, and standing kickbacks and never—like the others—getting his face wet.

Finally, when there was something going on everywhere but at Maxwell's booth, Francine took a deep breath, smiled, handed over one ticket, and closed her eyes. She felt his hand drift to her face and tilt her head just so,

"You're beautiful," he murmured, and then he kissed her. Something inside, a personal ice age, perhaps, melted just a little. She turned away, dazed, and got back in line.

Barbara stepped up, and Maxwell said, "This should help quell the dread," and he put his lips—moist and slightly citrus-flavored—on hers. She, too, returned to the end of the line.

When it was her turn, Judith heard arias, Susan started to weep, Aimee put her arms around Maxwell and had to be pulled gently away. The line grew long and restless. Small things were unpeeled. Larger things rose from a long sleep. A silence fell over the community room.

No one could get enough. Everyone wanted to be kissed, really kissed, again and again. Kim, who had quit smoking years ago, lit up a Marlboro. Lucia fell to her knees and thanked Saint Anthony, patron of lost things. The temperature in the room rose steadily.

Finally the men put a stop to it. They led their disheveled wives away, then came back for the others and took them, too, even though they resisted. Rex swore at Maxwell, and the other men glared menacingly. They threatened to meet Maxwell in the parking lot. Soon he was alone and he, being last, turned off the lights as he left.

FULL OF SHADOWS,
WITHOUT SUNLIGHT OR HOPE

Because Dr. Atkinson was a renowned scholar—widely read, widely published, widely envied, widely reviled—he was pleased to find himself in Hades.

His wife had followed his orders and placed a bolus—the traditional silver coin—on his lips during the last moments of his life. Now he held the coin tightly in one hand and stepped aside as the dazed pushed past him, cringing at Cerberus with his three heads, pressing money into Charon's grimy hand, then stumbling aboard the ferry.

Hades was just as he had always described it: dark, foul, and bituminous. Cerberus's mane consisted of serpents, Charon was gaunt and sour, the Acheron—not the Styx!—smoked and heaved. He squinted and looked west, then north. The Asphodel Meadows and Elysium couldn't be too far away. He'd drawn maps of the Underworld himself, and they introduced nearly every significant text.

As the shades stumbled past him, he went over his plan. He would remain here with the newly dead for a while. They were interesting, and he would never see them again after they'd been assigned to one terrible realm or another. Senior citizens staggered past—some in hospital gowns, others in ridiculous golfing togs. There were many of the middle-aged felled in their prime, one or two holding a spatula and wearing an apron entreating everyone to KISS THE COOK. And of course teenagers, shatterproof glass still embedded in their foreheads.

Jostled by the crowds, he gripped the bolus tightly. Without it he would wander this desolate shore for a hundred years. Once across the Acheron, though, his plan was foolproof: Heracles, Odysseus, even Orpheus had been to Hades and returned to the light, to a world of summer dresses on impressionable or desperate co-eds. He knew he was as intelligent as

Odysseus and Heracles, and Orpheus was just a guitar player much like the one to whom he'd given a C because he was young and handsome.

Dr. Atkinson planned his triumphant return from the dead: the articles he would write, the speeches he would give, the supple who would hang on every word.

Right now, he could wander among these poor souls unmolested. They were stunned by death and by death's environs. He almost felt like explaining, "Those moans come from the Cocytus, the river of lamentation. And the shrieks and swearing from the Styx, river of hate." But he didn't. Could they even hear him? And if they could, would they listen? He hated it when people didn't listen.

His musings carried him to a bend in the Acheron and a little beyond. It was there he saw something for which he was unprepared: children. Toddlers, mostly, in little overalls and shorts, some barefoot, some in tennies or slippers with bunny ears, a few in colorful bucket hats and sunglasses that were inevitably, comically, too large.

An involuntary cry escaped his dry and nearly always pursed lips. This was nowhere in the texts!

A hideous teenager, no doubt Charon's son, stood beside a snarling cur as child after child tottered onto a flimsy raft after handing over not a coin but a toy. A red ball, a Matchbox Car, a Zhu Zhu hamster, a doll, and—here is the one that made the professor stumble backwards in horror—a toy piano upon which the terribly burned child played the first few notes of the "Happy Birthday" song before it was torn from his grasp.

"Oh, God!" Professor Atkinson moaned backing away in horror, losing his balance, and then his footing. Groping for anything to break his fall, the bolus flew from his hand. A dozen skeletal forms fell on it, but only one rose with it between bony fingers and disappeared into the ever-present smoke. The rest returned to the zombie-like shuffle that would last a century. And Dr. Atkinson, pleading incoherently and weeping as he had never wept before, joined them.

WHY WE BROKE UP

We're parked at this turnout halfway up Angeles Crest. Couple of cars here and there. Windows steamed up. I'm with Brenda. I love her name. It sounds nourishing. We're both virgins. We both wear abstinence rings. We usually discuss physical lustful temptation, and it mostly goes away. But that night, what people call the mysterious allure of sex was spilling all over us. Brenda's all squirmy, and Brenda's never squirmy. Then she whispers, "Let's pretend."

We pretend to do it. We pretend we're sated. I pretend to smoke. She pretends to nag me about it. I pretend to get mad. She says she's only concerned about my health. I say she's always at me about something. She tells me not to wake the kids. I tell her I'll do any goddamned thing I want. She gets out, slams the car door, and sobs.

I look out the window and wonder where things went wrong.

A GUIDE TO THE MOST
COMMON TOXINS

When she passed an exasperated nurse in the hall, Judy knew she was close to her mother's room.

"Finally!" Laura said, dropping the remote.

"I was working, Mother. Work is love made visible."

"Bullshit. Work is hard on your hands. And I could have died. I was burning up with fever."

"One hundred and one is not dangerous."

"I felt so alone! Just like I did when you went to India. Of all places."

"Daddy was with you. And you were only having your boobs done."

"That's all men care about." She glanced at the TV where a tattooed couple swore at one another. "I don't suppose you have a boyfriend."

"Sangharakshita says that sexual relationships encourage neurotic dependence."

"Who said anything about sex? I'm talking about dinner at The Ivy. Sometimes I can't believe you're my daughter. It's like I did some retarded UPS man in my sleep."

"You actually were chronically unfaithful."

"I had needs, kiddo. Needs that weren't being met." She lowered her eyes.

"I'll never know how your father found all those men and got them to testify."

"It was in all the papers for weeks, Mother. Reporters wouldn't leave me alone. I had to move."

"From that piece-of-shit condo. Who cares?"

"And change my name."

"To Judy, for Jesus's sake. Why not Tanini or Dakota? Something with pizzazz. No successful man wants a Judy. It rhymes with fruity."

"I said that I wanted to be the change I wished to see in the world, so it started with my name. There are no mistakes."

Laura narrowed her heavily made-up eyes. "I really don't get you."

Judy patted her mother's hand. "I just try to keep a green bough in my heart so the singing bird will come."

"Jesus Christ. Where do you get that stuff? You sound like that quack chiropractor I was seeing. The one with the big kundalini. He could spout that crap for hours."

"Mother, I believe that if I speak with a polluted mind, suffering will follow."

Laura pulled her daughter closer. "Listen, Judy, or whatever your name is. I'm glad you're here even if you do sound completely batshit. I want to apologize for that incident with the iron when you were nine. I know it left a helluva scar, and you can't wear a bikini. I guess I was crying downstairs in Recovery, and when that nurse with the bad breath asked me if I was in pain, I said not from the operation; I just haven't been the best mother in the world. But you were just so noisy that morning, and I had such a hangover."

"I was playing solitaire."

"And slapping the cards down!"

Judy smiled at her mother. "Let's just say forgiveness is a gift I give myself."

Laura fell back on the pillows. "Get me some orange juice. I'm dizzy. I know I'm diabetic. I don't care what that big-nosed sawbones says."

Judy walked to the nurse's station where half a dozen cups of orange juice waited on a blue tray.

"Everything okay?" asked the nurse.

"Uh-huh."

"That mother of yours is really a piece of work. Funny thing is those are the kind that live forever."

A minute later, Laura took a sip of juice and scowled. "Too cold. Put it on the sill in the sun."

Judy went to the window, turned her back to the bed, and took the vial from her purse. She'd gone all the way to Uttranchal to buy it from a man with one arm and one eye.

Three drops went into the juice. It was slow-acting but lethal. Judy would be at work when the call came. She'd rehearsed shock and disbelief and looked forward to letting the phone drop from her hand as sympathetic coworkers rushed to her side.

WHATEVER IT TAKES

Sean pulled Melanie to him. "We're safe here behind this smoldering Volvo. That Necroborg didn't see us make a run for it. But don't look. It's too horrible."

"Is it hopeless, darling? So hopeless that we may as well throw off the chains of Judeo-Christian repression and act out our wildest fantasies?"

"You're very tempting in that ripped-in-all-the-right-places mini, but there are those weak signals from the south." He patted the radio at his side. "We should follow them before we indulge our baser impulses. There may be other survivors."

"Other men?"

"Many other men. Often in leather pants."

"Ever since aliens destroyed the greater Phoenix area six weeks ago, leaving three-quarters of the population dead and spawning a frightening array of zombies, all I can think about is how attractive you are unshaven with the sleeves ripped off your already distressed Abercrombie T-shirt."

"I can see the shattered windows of a supermarket. I wonder if there's anything left to eat. Ever since The Intensity, scavenging has been fierce and combative."

Melanie's hand crept under Sean's shirt. "I love it when you scavenge."

"I should secure the perimeter. But shattered glass is everywhere. And mannequins are still wearing those vapid smiles even though almost all their clothes have been torn off by filthy, calloused hands."

"Tell me about the mannequins again. That got me hot."

Sean holds out half a bottle of water. "This is the last of it. It'll be dark soon. And you know what darkness brings—more of them!"

Melanie guzzled, then threw the empty bottle away carelessly. "I hated recycling."

"I can hear them closing in, shuffling and snorting."

"Kiss me! Kiss me like it's the last time, and then . . ."

Just then the bedroom door flew open, and there stood one of the undead—partly decomposed, rotting, moist.

Sean shot to his feet. Melanie clung to one of his legs, planted wide like a Colossus. As Melanie screamed, Sean launched himself at the fiend. The struggle was brief. Soon Sean stood panting over the hideous body.

"There are more coming," he said. "I can hear them."

Melanie tore at her blouse, revealing a Victoria's Secret Demi-Underwire in Hot Pink/Black. "Take me, darling," she cried. "Take me now before it's too late."

Ten minutes later, as Melanie dozed, Sean crept out of bed and into the living room. There sat Nick, his costume already packed into a duffle.

Sean reached for his checkbook. "This is the awkward part."

Nick just smiled. "We're actors, we don't judge."

Sean wrote quickly, then stood up. "Do you get to go home now?" Nick glanced at the check. "Hey, man. Thanks. But no rest for the weary. About an hour from now I'm a sensitive poet who also just happens to be a master of passion, so I better hustle my buns. See you next time, I hope."

Nick opened the door. "Drive careful, okay? You never know what's out there."

HANSON AND GRETA

When I was in college, I didn't have the time or the money to date. In the daytime, I waited tables in a sorority, and at night I worked in a pharmacy. I always seemed to be on my knees filling shelves with maxi-pads when the prettiest girls came in.

I had friends who were girls, though. One or two from my French study group, one or two from the sorority where I worked. They'd pledged, then dropped out to live in the dorms.

It was one of the latter, Greta Arnold, who asked me to go with her to the clinic. Her boyfriend, a notorious Sigma Chi, was, she said, hopeless, and she wanted nothing to do with him. "C'mon, Hanson, be a pal."

Because I walked everywhere or took the bus, I enjoyed driving her car, a BMW just a few years old. Business was brisk at the clinic. Two girls sat side by side flipping through a tattered magazine. They showed each other pictures of celebrities and called them names. A pale girl with tri-colored hair sat by her mother who glared at me. The only other male was a Hispanic kid with a shaved head and clear, terrified eyes. His girlfriend sat with both arms across her breasts and exuded an air of great sexual regret.

Greta was having the procedure when a mother emerged with her daughter who was so pale her blue eyes looked like chips of tanzanite dropped in snow. As she groped for the door, her mother stopped long enough to snarl at me, "Use your head next time, Stupid." I was nervous, and I laughed. Then she slapped me.

At 3:30 p.m. I drove Greta home, stopping along the way for a chili dog, which she devoured, then promptly threw up. I helped her to her room and got her some water. "You're sweet," she said, kissing me on the cheek. Her breath smelled metallic.

A few weeks later, a girl I didn't know stopped me by the Science Building, introduced herself as Beth, and said, "I'm a friend of Greta's. Want to take a ride with me on Friday? Looks like I got bit by the pants leg snake."

Our destination turned out to be a medical building downtown. On the way, Beth said, "I was Wendy in high school. In *Peter Pan*, I mean. J.M. Barrie is probably pretty disappointed in me."

This waiting room was blue with a huge aquarium along the north wall. The fish were sluggish, and drab as Mormons. A nurse offered me bottled water. I read a very literate article about how fireflies blink to attract mates. Eventually Beth came out and used her Visa card.

She was woozy, and we walked slowly toward the elevator. Halfway there, she stopped and leaned against me. Automatically I put my arms around her.

"You bastard," she sobbed, "you creepy, crummy bastard. Keep your fucking hands to yourself."

The next time a stranger asked me for a date, I said that I was very busy. When one persisted, I said that my name was Hanson, but I wasn't that Hanson.

I couldn't be alone in my room, so I went to bars, put my quarter on the pool table or my name on the chalk board. I played badly, so I was courted by the feral stickmen with their personalized cues. I liked the chivalry of eight ball. I liked the juke box turned as high as it would go.

WAR

He comes back reciting the poetry of war. Not that crap from high school, those stupid roads diverging. The real poetry of war. It recites itself to him, and he recites it back.

He'd like to give a rat's ass about the night school teachers and bartenders his wife has been sleeping with. He'd like to get all riled up and crash his new pickup. But he's busy listening to the poetry of war, which nobody else can hear.

His mother just sucks it up and cooks. His father is fucking hopeless. Crying when those busses pulled up to the Ramada two years ago, and now Dad's—what's that word?—baffled. Yeah. Fuck.

Then one day at the mall, there's this girl at the Hospitality Desk. Plain. Staring at a book maybe because everybody knows where The Gap Outlet is, and half the other stores are closed.

And he manages to put together a sentence. "What are you reading?"

"Something," she says, "sufficiently sordid to keep me from falling asleep."

Sufficiently sordid. Even the poetry of war stopped to listen.

Her nametag said "Ivy" and he knew, from a life before this one, how ivy could, in time, bring down any wall.

"Is that your real name?" he asks.

"What happened to your face?" she answers.

BFF

Caroline paced the living room. What was wrong with Isabella? Why had she moved to the Weird Kids table? They used to make fun of Fedora and Joshitha and Ummi. So why was she sitting there eating tofu with them and laughing hysterically.

Frustrated, Caroline picked up a copy of her dad's *Journal of Nanotechnology*. Flipping through at random, she saw this full-page ad:

Lia is the perfect sidekick. Cute but not cuter
than you. A little shorter than you. Lots of pizzazz
but not as much as you. Cool clothes but not
as cool as yours. Boys love to talk to Lia about
you. She automatically texts you ten times
a day and can be programmed for twice that.

Lia can't say anything crappy about your
new low-rise jeans. It's impossible for her
to borrow your blue cardigan, go out with LeBron,
then bring it back with something icky on
the sleeve.

Stacey is a real best friend. You two spend
every second together until Tyler gets out of math
and then she "sleeps." If you have a zit, she has
two. If you get dizzy using a tampon, she
totally passes out. She is the world's best
listener and if you want to talk all night,
she would never go to sleep and snore like
you-know-who.

Lia and Stacey are loyal and celibate. Their
compliments are sincere and additional ones
can be purchased online.

What are you waiting for? There are payment plans
in every price range.

Excited, Caroline went to the computer and right to her Mom's One-
Click Account.

JUST LOOKING

A creepy old man wanders into the Guess! store. Dawn, who has been pricing cashmere gloves and puzzling over last night's sales figures, watches him smooth Egyptian cotton with his bony fingers, then hold up a T-shirt.

"What's with the cloak?" she whispers to Amber.

"I know," says Amber. "Hoods are so last year."

"He, like, smells bad. Thank God you're up."

Amber will talk to anybody, and she's a bit of a tease. She minces up to the creepy old man and asks if she can be of any assistance.

He eyes Amber and then Dawn. But he's not like most guys. Not at all like most guys.

He croaks, "I'm just looking."

Amber isn't tops in sales because she's shy. "Check this out!" she says holding up a sweater. "You don't want to be the world's oldest Goth, do you? This Heritage half-zip cable knit is great for the active guy. And the turquoise really makes your eyes pop!"

All of a sudden, the creepy old man looks at his watch, an ancient timepiece with an insistent tick-tock-tick.

"Another time, my dear. Right now I have an appointment."

Amber gives him her card and he rushes out.

She is totally shameless! Not two days ago, Dawn let Amber kiss her in the stock room, and now look! Dawn is about to say something, about to remind Amber of that kiss and what it meant. Or might mean. Or should mean. She marches right to Amber, who is standing in the door now. Before she can say anything, Amber's arm slips around Dawn's waist. Amber's fragrant hair falls onto Dawn's shoulder.

"Get a room!" shouts a boy on a skateboard as he collides with a parking meter and falls bleeding and unconscious not right at their feet, but almost.

LOIS LANE'S SECRET DIARY

Here's the thing about kryptonite: it's a little harder to handle than I thought. I made this tincture to calm Superman down. I don't always want to get my hair all messed up flying to Pittsburgh. Sometimes I just want to stay home. So I dabbed a little behind my ears. S. came in from deflecting another meteorite, and when he gave me a hug I held on. Pretty soon he said, "Jeez, I'm just pooped all of a sudden. What if we rent a DVD and just stay home?" Perfect! While I cooked dinner, he took a nap on the couch. Even that little curl that my girlfriends think is so cute relaxed. He even snored!

But after dinner, he wouldn't dry the pots and pans or take out the garbage. (Usually he just breathed on the dish rack and launched the trash into deep space!) That's when I heard myself say, "Do I have to do everything around here?" God, I sounded like my mother. I was ashamed of what I'd done and vowed to never do it again.

Except I did. I'd had a really busy week at the *Daily Planet*. I've never seen such a crime-ridden city! And S. was everywhere—sucking up that oil spill just off Galveston and battling the Atomic Skull. And to make matters worse, the undead were back! I'd send Jimmy out for a bagel just to keep my blood sugar up, and he'd return as a zombie. And no bagel!!

Friday night, I picked up some Chinese takeout and hoped S. wouldn't be home when I got there. I needed a little me-time. But there he was, and of course, he's hot to trot. Saving the world gives him a woodie. I tell him to just give me a minute, and when I come out of the bathroom, I've got tincture of kryptonite spritzed everywhere.

We start to make out, and then he says he feels dizzy. I tell him, "Sit down, sweetheart." And I lead him to the couch. He's in his civvies, and there's a stain on his shirt. He looks up at me and croaks, "I fuckin' hate my life sometimes, you know that?" I start to cry. S. never swears! He stands up, fists clenched. "Shut up," he yells. "Shut up or I'll really give you something to cry about!"

That's when I grabbed a coat and ran out of the house. He found me a few hours later at the Motel 6. He'd stepped outdoors for some air and his X-ray vision kicked in. He didn't remember much. "What happened?" he asked.

He's almost fine now; the other day he adjusted longitude, then caught a bus full of paralyzed orphans as it plunged off a cliff. But sometimes he comes home and forgets to give me a kiss. He opens a beer and watches the Weather Channel. And once a week or so I'll wake up, and he'll be standing at the window staring into the dark.

Oh, dear diary—what have I done?

LOUP-GAROU

Every morning Margot and Walter had coffee and All-Bran in silence. His raised newspaper and hers formed a kind of corridor through which passed the ghosts of children they never had, the RV they'd talked about but couldn't afford, the friends who had stopped dropping by due to Walter's excoriating, bellicose opinions about everything.

Every evening a tasteless dinner made even less palatable by the UFO glow of the TV. Both of them in the twin Barcaloungers he'd found at Veteran's Thrift and repaired with duct tape.

But once a month, every month, he put on his hat, said good-bye and didn't return until morning.

"What do you do out there?" she asked one night. "I used to think you had a girlfriend but not anymore. No sane woman would have you."

He turned around then. Leaning against the wall he said, "You think you're so smart. You really want to know? You're not going to like it."

"Try me."

"I'm a werewolf."

Margot stared, then started to laugh. She wallowed in her chair, pitching from side to side. She laughed so hard she honked and snorted.

He pointed, "I'm just gonna go in the spare room." He rotated his big head painfully. "You don't need to see the change. But when I come out, I'll be a wolf. Maybe the sight of that'll shut you up. Leave this door open so I can get outdoors. I don't want to have to jump through a window. But I could if I wanted to."

Margot limped into the kitchen and found a beer in the old refrigerator. She chuckled, blew her nose, and wiped at her eyes. *Werewolf.* She sat at the kitchen table and looked at the ads. Good-looking, young people pointing to things she couldn't afford. Dusk melted to dark. A huge, round moon bullied its way among the stars.

Then she heard the clack of claws on hard wood and heard a low growl. When she turned there he was, fangs showing.

"Walter?"

The wolf bolted for the outdoors and was gone. Margot hobbled to the old Dodge and followed him.

Oh, my god. The look of him as he ran—the long, lean sleekness of him, the delight he took in clearing the decrepit picket fence, the way he stopped and drank his reflection in a puddle of standing water, the cold yellow eyes he turned on her, long red tongue dangling.

Then he howled, turned his back, and bounded into the woods. The forest deep and dark. Margot let the little car coast, then stop. *Unbelievable*. She could hardly wait for morning.

"Bite me," she said.

Walter looked up from his cereal. The bags under his eyes were, if possible, darker than ever. The creases in his forehead deeper.

She repeated herself. "Isn't that how it works? A werewolf bites somebody and then she's a werewolf, too? Please. It's something we could do together. And to be able to run like that . . . It must be wonderful."

"No. Your breath stinks."

"I don't want you to kiss me. I want you to bite me so—"

"Nope. I like things the way they are."

"Walter, that's just mean and selfish."

He pretended to lap milk from his bowl. "Well, that's the beast in me, ain't it."

That afternoon while Walter was napping, Margot made her way to Todd's Gun Shop. She waited her turn, then whispered to Todd.

"You're kidding," he said lowering his voice. "Nobody carries silver bullets."

"Could you make one?"

He frowned. "Well, I might be able to find some old reenactor who'd give it a try, but—"

She interrupted him. "Let's do that," she said. "I only need one. And tell him money is no object."

SCATTERED CLOUDS AND SUN

"Bob your friendly weatherman here, friends. Today we find ourselves just outside Phoenix at the gated community of Nuevo Antiguo. We're talking to Sarah Barber about what some folks around here are calling a new utopia. Sarah, can you tell us a little bit about this phenomenon?"

"Well, Bob, a while ago a bunch of us women were having lunch and wondering what we could do to help out Sheila Bradford's husband, Will. Sheila's sick, and Will is just about worn down from taking care of her. Somebody said it's a shame Curtis Soebell couldn't step in. He's a born caretaker. Then Will could sleep with Curtis's wife, Molly, who's a real firecracker and way too much woman for Curtis, anyway."

"What was the weather like that day, Sarah?"

"Slightly overcast but warm. And even warmer once we got to talking."

"Tell us about what happened next."

"Maybe it was the mimosas, but Pammy Bass said she'd like to have somebody new to talk to. Her husband is tired of stories about the grandkids or which nursing home to put her mom in, but if she had somebody else's husband, he'd listen after they had sex. And they would have sex because they hadn't been married for forty years.

"So I said, 'Why don't we just tell the boys that they can park in any driveway they like tonight, and let's see what happens.'"

"Holy cow, Sarah. I'll bet those men couldn't wait for the sun to set at 6:37."

"You can say that again, Bob. The gals cooked dinners from scratch and took showers, and the boys came straight home from work or the golf course."

"And no problems to speak of? No, shall we say, stormy weather?"

"Not to speak of, Bob. We only had one rule—a different driveway every night. Sure, men are men and they were all dying for a look at Jo Beth's boobs, but after a month or so a brute like Steve Diamond just wanted to give Sheila Bradford a bath and read to her. And by the way, Sheila got better, too."

"All's well that ends well. Thanks, Sarah. That's all we have time for today, so goodbye from Nuevo Antiguo where it's seventy-three, looking for a high of eighty-six. Now back to the studio."

MOTHERS & DAUGHTERS

There I stand with my torch. The torch I used to search for Persephone after she was abducted by Hades. Raped, actually. Stolen and raped and hidden away. And did anybody help me find her? All they did was whine: "Demeter, I'm hungry." "Demeter, what happened to the rain?" "Demeter, why is the wheat falling over on itself?"

Everybody could starve for all I care. I had Persephone's picture on every half gallon of milk in the world. I was tireless. I didn't eat, I didn't sleep. All I did was search.

As it turned out, my innocent little daughter liked sleeping with the enemy. So I had to imagine Hades's filthy hands on her white flesh. Don't you think she did that to spite me? After all I've done. The sacrifices I've made.

All I ever wanted was for her to be safe forever. We'd be sisters for eternity— borrowing each other's clothes and gossiping. Everybody on Olympus would ask, "Which one is the daughter? They're both so beautiful!"

What I got instead is a few months with her in the summer and even then it's Hades-this and Hades-that.

I really cannot bear to think about it.

• • • • • • • • • • •

Everyone knows that fairytale about the seasons—Hades took me, my mother's sorrow knew no bounds, blah blah blah. Here's the naked truth. I was my mother's hostage. Her toy. A pet she let loose briefly to gather flowers with her playmates. I had suitors—Ares and Apollo to name just two—but she rejected them and sent me to gather more crocuses.

Then one day Hades rose out of the earth, put a sooty hand around my ankle and I woke up in the underworld. Did I weep? At first. Was I afraid? Who wouldn't be. But Hades was patient. While Mother wandered and wept and basically said, "Look at me! Look at me!" Hades and I played tag in the Elysian Fields and cruised the rivers. He showed me off to the damned. (Tantalus said that the sight of me was like pineapple on his tongue!) Eventually he pulled me down and kissed me. His lips tasted like iron. Dark blood I didn't know I had coursed through my innocent veins, and I heard myself gasp, "Kiss me again."

I learned to love my new kingdom. My husband has a helmet of darkness that makes the owner invisible. I put it on, tip-toe around him, pull on his beard, and blow in his ear. When I take it off, I'm wearing only a few jewels. I play with Cerberus and stroll through the fields of Asphodel. Just the sight of me, just a whiff of my fragrant hair makes the poor souls suffer more for what might have been. When I tell Hades I've been tormenting the damned, he laughs and kisses me all over.

I knew it couldn't last. My mother got Zeus involved and the next thing I know it's six months with her. Well, I know how to wait. I admit Mother's world can be pleasant with its orchestras and Italian restaurants.

But I prefer the underworld where I am more than just a pretty girl, more than Demeter's stunning daughter. There I am a dark queen, and people fear me.

NEGATIVE SPACE

My dad taught me to pack: lay out everything. Put back half. Roll things that roll. Wrinkle-prone things on top of cotton things. Then pants, waist-to-hem. Nooks and crannies for socks. Belts around the sides like snakes. Plastic over that. Add shoes. Wear heavy stuff on the plane.

We started when I was little. I'd roll up socks. Then he'd pretend to put me in the suitcase, and we'd laugh. Some guys bond with their dads shooting hoops or talking about Chevrolets. We did it over luggage.

By the time I was twelve, if he was busy, I'd pack for him. Mom tried but didn't have the knack. He'd get somewhere, open his suitcase and text me—"Perfect." That one word from him meant a lot.

The funeral was terrible—him laid out in that big carton and me crying and thinking, *Look at all that wasted space.*

OFFICE HOURS 10–11 MWF

Oliver Oliver sat in the uncomfortable chair and waited until I'd finished circling the mistakes on someone's quiz. He picked up a pen, then put it down, picked up a see-through paperweight, then put it down. Picked up the pen again and slipped it into the top pocket of his green shirt.

"So," he began, "Dr. Koertge—"

"I'm not a doctor."

"But if you were, what kind would you be? Gynecologist maybe?"

"Your parents must have a real sense of humor."

"How so?"

"Oliver Oliver."

"All the men in my family are named Oliver Oliver."

"That must make for an interesting Thanksgiving."

"Intonation does it. You know by the way your wife or your sister or your mother says the name which Oliver she means. It's kind of like the Chinese language where a word pronounced one way means *bread* and pronounced another way it means *fuck you*."

"We have class in a few minutes, Mr. Oliver."

"Don't be formal. Call me by my first name."

"What's on your mind, Oliver?"

"It's about your class. I don't think you should teach a word like *deliquesce*."

"It's a vocabulary class."

"To girls, I mean. If it was just dudes and studs and beefcake, that'd be okay."

"*Deliquesce* means to melt."

"Are you serious? I thought it meant to, you know, ejaculate."

"You never listen. You sit in the back with your iPod turned so high the other students complain."

He stood up. "Melt, huh. Well, thanks for clearing that up."
As he turned away I reminded him, "That's my pen in your pocket."
He made a sound that might have qualified as Chinese.
"We're out of bread," I told him. "Come back tomorrow."

TURNER CLASSIC MOVIES:
ON DANGEROUS GROUND

In the first ten minutes, Robert Ryan gets in hot water. Some two-bit thug almost died from the beating Ryan gave him. *I got the guy to come clean, didn't I?*

Okay, okay. He'll go upstate for a while and help out some hick sheriff.

In the city, the streets are always dark and wet, but in Pokeyville there's nothing but light and, every undergrad's favorite symbol, snow. Fields of it. Immaculate.

Robert Ryan doesn't phone it in. He's too much of a pro for that. But except for what the director does with shadows, it's just a job. Money in the bank.

Ryan clocks out at five o'clock, drives home down Sunset, hustlers at every corner. He remembers enough Keats to mutter, "What men or gods are these?"

At home, he chats with his wife, Jessica Cadwalader, while she fixes dinner. Small talk. They've been married a long time. The kids are grown. She's still pretty though.

His hand tightens around his highball glass. What does she do, he wonders, all by herself, day after day, in this rotten town?

PERFECT COPIES

When her phone rang, Melanie picked up and heard, "There's a Tony here asking for you. Can I send him back?"

Melanie sighed as she pinned a colorful travel brochure on the cork board in her cubicle. Tahiti. Another place she'd never go.

She smiled and led Tony to the copy machine. She watched him uncap the toner. She'd known him for a decade. That pleasant smile. Those clear, blue eyes. The same blue polo shirt with the Perfect Copies logo. She had aged. Gracefully, but she had. While he did not look a day older.

Could it be?

Impulsively she went to her supervisor and said she didn't feel well. She endured another pat on the ass before she hurried downstairs and followed Tony to his van. She stayed a block behind, accompanying him on his rounds. Three more stops at three different companies. Then a short drive through an industrial park before he pulled up to a guard and said something before he was waved through.

The guard, despite the uniform, looked exactly like Tony.

Melanie waited. The lot was packed with identical vans, each one with Perfect Copies on the side. In a decade, the company had nearly replaced Xerox with quality machines and astonishingly prompt service.

Exactly at 5:00 p.m., a single Lexus cruised out of the gate. The guard saluted, the driver waved and headed out of the city. Melanie followed in her white Corolla. Forty minutes later, she was in a subdivision—red tile roofs, two-car garages, pristine lawns.

When the Lexus pulled into the driveway at 5500 Tweedledum Terrace, she parked a block away. Melanie was so excited. There was so much she wanted to do. So many places she wanted to see. She was forty-five. Not old. All she needed was time.

Just then, Tony came around the side of the house. He was dressed in jeans, T-shirt, low muddy boots. He pushed a wheelbarrow crisscrossed with a hoe and a rake, like some huge coat of arms.

Breathing deeply and as evenly as she could, Melanie started the car, drove right up in front of the house, parked deliberately, and got out. Beneath her feet, the grass was like a cushion. She went right up to Tony. This Tony.

"Do you remember me?" she asked.

He leaned on the rake. "Of course. You're from the office on Wilshire."

"Do you know why I'm here."

"No."

"I want to see the original."

"I'm afraid I don't understand." Tony turned away to rake around the base of the crepe myrtle tree. He made perfect, wavy lines. Like in a Zen garden she'd seen on TV.

"I'm not leaving," she said firmly. "I may not look it but I am, in my own modest way, a desperate character."

Just then the front door opened. She turned and there he was—Tony. The real Tony. And, oh thank God, ten years older. Gray at the temples, a little soft here and there. But throbbing with vitality.

"You know what I want," she said. "Just one. She could go to work and I could finally enjoy—"

"I understand completely, Melanie. I always liked you. I was just so busy in the lab." He opened the door wider. "Please come in."

"I have money," she said. "Some, anyway."

"That won't be necessary." He stood aside as she passed and warmth washed over her. "The pleasure of seeing more of you will be payment enough."

PLURAL PRONOUN

"Class, listen up!" "Class, turn to page two forty-one." "Class, settle down." Class this. Class that.

We weren't Bill and Javier, Sonia, Ben and Louis, Michael, Idris, Lisa, Karl, Todd, Davey, Amalio, Justin, Nila, Gerry, Ed, Alicia, Steph, Micah, Cyan, Sara, JD, and Will anymore. We were one thing. An entity.

Fine. So be it. We'd been raised to value individuality even as each of us trudged to The Gap and bought identical clothes. Then we realized that whereas one blue polo and one pair of white linen pants identifies the wearer as a feckless dupe who wants desperately to fit in, two dozen blue polos and two dozen pairs of white linen pants are formidable.

Thus attired, we returned to the classroom. When one of us was called on, we all went to the board. When we yawned, the windows fogged over. Assigned to write about Free Will, we handed in the same essay.

"Who is the plagiarist?" she demanded as her kitschy mood ring pulsed spasmodically.

We raised all our hands.

"Are you trying to drive me mad?" she howled.

"No." We answered in unison as our teacher ran screaming from the room.

WESTERN UNION

I got home from school, and there was this telegram on the table. A real telegram. Yellow and everything. Addressed to me. I thought it was a joke. Or a cool invitation to a party or something.

FELICIA MAKE HAY WHILE THE SUN SHINES STOP CARPE SOME DIEM STOP HAVE YOU GOT SOME PURPLE DANCING SHOES STOP I'D PUT THEM ON STOP I KNOW YOURE JUST VEGAN TO UPSET YOUR MOM STOP HAVE SOME RIBS CHICAGO-STYLE STOP THIS IS NOT PERSONAL FELICIA STOP ITS JUST WHAT I DO STOP I GET ON THE BUS IN THE MORNING TO GO TO WORK STOP I PUT MY LITTLE BOX OF DARKNESS DOWN BY MY SHOES STOP DID YOU KNOW I SPEAK 160 LANGUAGES STOP SO I MIGHT CALL YOUR NAME AND YOU WOULDN'T UNDERSTAND STOP YOU MIGHT THINK IT WAS JUST ANOTHER CRAZY GUY OUTSIDE STARBUCKS ACTING OUT

Seriously? What kind of sick person would do this? I threw it away. But I couldn't stop thinking about it. Probably I ought to tell somebody. My dad knows some cops. I'll bet they could find out who sent it. When I went back to the little waste can by the mail table, it wasn't there. I was the only one in the house, too. I thought, *Great. Now nobody will believe me.*

I stayed away from Starbucks, that's for sure. Some time went by. I didn't forget, but I didn't obsess either. I even thought, *Maybe I should have a little more fun? Maybe I should give Mom a break?* So I do, and guess what— it worked.

Then I'm meeting Jill downtown at some new place, and when I get off the train and turn the first corner, there's a Starbucks and a homeless guy out in front giving some dude in a suit a hard time, and when he sees me, he stops and fumbles in his backpack, and I think, *Oh, no!*

PRACTICAL ASPECTS OF
POLYGAMY

"Tina! Tina! Can I have another glass of water? With lemon this time?"

Tina puts both hands over her ears. She's trying to watch this TV show about plural marriage—a moderator and a red-haired man with his six wives. Wife number five says, "We all have our roles, but when it gets to be a little too much around the house with the kids and all, then somebody else takes over."

Tina would like Water Wife to step right up. Water Wife with Lemon. Who could relieve Nurse Wife who's been changing the sheets while The Husband suffers through influenza. Chef Wife makes nourishing broth. Sex Wife sits out in the sun getting a yummy color. For later.

Sometimes Tina would like to be Sex Wife, usually after an afternoon TV movie with lots of ads about rugged trucks and the men who drive them.

The moderator asks, "What about sex?"

Wife number three says, "One of our duties is to rear children."

"Right. But what about sex?"

Two says, "He makes love to all of us."

"At the same time?"

"Of course not! He's a married man."

Tina can hear the thrashing of the bedclothes.

"Where's my lemon water?"

She goes into the backyard and pretends she is married to the red-haired man. Today she is Outdoor Wife. Inside are five or six women who love her even though she's the prettiest. The house is always warm and clean. Obedient children in another room. When all the wives go to the store together, they walk in a line like ducklings.

"Tina! Goddammit!"

She wonders if the other wives ever sleep together. Not in a sleazy, daytime TV way, but a nice way. Cozy and warm. Any kind of ruckus and someone else gets up. Whispers to her, "I'll go. You rest, you sweet thing."

PRINCIPLES OF HANDICAPPING

A periodical called *Daily Racing Form* publishes past performances of every registered thoroughbred. Gamblers consult these brief histories to see how a horse they are thinking of betting on has performed in the past.

For example, a filly named Teen Age Temptress prefers weekends to weekdays. Past performances show that she tends to sulk and toss her rider on Wednesdays, Thursdays, and Fridays. Thus no savvy bettor would be attracted to Teen Age Temptress on any weekday afternoon.

I am a student of past performances, so am not alarmed when Sheila brings her revolver to the breakfast table on Sunday morning. She has done this before and ended up sobbing and penitent in my arms.

Still, there are always variables in handicapping. A sudden storm, for example, might change the track conditions. Or whispers from the denizens of the backstretch with new and startling information. I begin thinking fast since the grim set of Sheila's jaw is certainly a new variable.

PYGMIES OF THE RAIN FOREST

The nurses told Barry it didn't mean anything when his mother was moved to the third floor of St. Mary's Hospital, but he knew that it was a place for really sick people.

The room was nicer, though. Bigger and brighter. A more comfortable chair for him to sit in and do homework or read as his mother drifted in and out of sleep.

There was even a prettier picture to stare at. The ones downstairs were so swirly, and they didn't seem to be pictures of anything. This new one showed a real place—a lake. A big lake. Reeds up close to the shore, three ducks taking off, one after another like planes out of LAX. He stood up close. The ducks were pretty realistic—pale chests and dark blue heads with kind of white chinstraps.

Because his teachers heard what had happened to his mother, they were easy on him. Even the bullies cut him some slack because everybody knew. He did overhear one of the girls in his class whisper that her father said Barry's mother had "one foot in the grave."

That made Barry kind of sick. He saw his mother not lying down anymore but in an awkward and embarrassing position. He concentrated on the painting instead. He pretended he was there standing up to his knees in the cool water. His mom was on a blanket, watching him. The ducks weren't afraid. In fact, they ate bread right from his hand.

Two days after his mother had been moved upstairs—it was a Wednesday, and Barry's report on Pygmies of the Rainforest was due—the nice nurse, Monica, took him aside and said that his mother was all right, but the lady next door in 2013 had passed away.

Inside his mother's room, he straightened her blankets, kissed her on the cheek, and patted her hand. She smelled funny. Not like she used to at all.

He went to the window, envying the cars leaving, maybe with somebody kind of pale and thin but basically okay and glad to be outdoors again.

Then he stared at the painting. So peaceful. He could almost feel the water on his legs, the lake's squishy bottom. He whispered, "Hi, ducks." He looked at one, then another, then . . . Wait. There were only two now. He must have counted wrong, and who could blame him. He had a lot on his mind. Everybody said so.

Thursday the doctor talked to him and said it was a good sign that his mother wasn't worse. It meant she was holding her own. But it was a bad sign that she hadn't improved.

On his way out of the hospital, Monica and an orderly in green scrubs rushed past him and disappeared into the room right across from his mother's. Barry went cold all over. Instead of going right to his aunt's house, he rode the elevator all the way to the cafeteria where he waited, stirring the icky pudding he bought but had no intention of eating. Sad-looking people came and went or talked on their phones in hushed tones.

An hour or so later he crept back upstairs. The room across the hall was empty. In his mother's room there was only one duck in the painting.

He stepped closer to the canvas. He leaned in and studied the surface inch by inch. He was sure he was missing something. And then—there it was! A tiny figure in the reeds. Just a torso. But a torso holding a gun.

Barry dashed to the nurses' station and borrowed a pen from Monica. He drew a tiny figure not far from the hunter. Another torso, dark-skinned and bare-chested. Holding a blow gun and inside that a poisoned dart.

When he'd finished, he kissed his mother good-bye, strolled to the elevator, and—downstairs—unlocked his bike. He wasn't in a hurry now. The weather was gorgeous. He was sure when he got home his aunt would run to him and say, "Oh, honey. The hospital just called. Your mother is out of danger!"

He would act surprised and let her hug him. He would never spoil the good news by saying that he already knew.

THE RAPE

They'd agreed to go to the arboretum on Sunday. To save time, he'd pick Leda up at the spa where she worked.

When he opened the door, a muscular trainer in a GET RIPPED tank top started a sales pitch about membership plans until Micah said he was just there to pick up Leda.

"So you're the lucky one," said the trainer whose name tag read, "Rich." "Every guy in this place has been trying to get next to her. She's an odd one but, man, what a body!"

A minute later she came out of the dressing room looking radiant and fresh in jeans and a white blouse.

Micah was so flattered by what Rich had said that he didn't mind riding in silence. The usual uneasy silence, but at least she let her hand rest on his shoulder.

Micah hadn't been to the arboretum since he was a child. He'd forgotten how huge it was. Hills and hidden places. Glens and vales and fountains. An enormous lake, waterfalls, winding paths. Geese and ducks and swans.

They walked slowly. He remembered being younger, dating girls from high school who wore shorts and flip-flops. Goofing around with them, killing time till they could make out.

Micah turned to Leda. Tugged her close to him.

"Don't," Leda said pulling away. "Let's sit down."

Leda chose an empty bench near the lake. They had to make their way to it over wet ground that was roughed up. In turmoil almost. Like the scene of a struggle.

He was used to her silences and, anyway, he was distracted by the swans that paddled toward them looking, he thought, for a handout. Two then six, nine then twelve, an armada of swans. Unblinking and focused. On them.

"There's something you should know," Leda said finally. "I'm named after the woman Zeus raped."

"I guessed. I know that story."

"It's more than a story. It happened to my ancestor."

He tried to touch her black, shiny hair, but she pulled away, reached for her purse, and took out a scroll bound by black ribbon.

"This," she said, "is a letter from Leda to her husband Tyndareus." And then she read: "'Beloved, it will be better for both of us if we part. It is not fair to you. Zeus has ruined me. The stench of him, the punishing bill, the huge wings. Forgive me, seek out a simpler woman, and live in peace.'"

Micah felt the anger in his stomach. "What's going on, Leda?"

She showed him the letter written in a strange language.

"Anybody," he said, "can buy that parchment-looking paper from Staples. You're breaking up with me. Jesus, Leda. I was going to kiss you, not rape you. How long have we been going out? You never want to do anything."

"I thought you were different. I thought you might understand."

"I understand all right. You're a tease and you're crazy. Man, if I was the kind of guy you think I am, I'd slap the crap out of you." He took both hands out of his pockets. "And maybe that's what you want, huh? Maybe you're that kind of—"

He couldn't finish because—neck stretched, tendons rigid, hissing in a language he couldn't hope to understand—she spoke to the swans.

And they came for him, all of them. He ran, and at first the spectators laughed, but that soon stopped and turned to shrieks as the huge birds covered him, tearing at his clothes, muffling his screams with their huge, white wings.

MONSTERS AT THEIR LEISURE

Wolfman chasing a red ball. Dracula in a polo shirt. Frankenstein playing badminton. The Banshee humming as she does dishes. Grendel's mother sunning on the deck at Dark Lake. Medusa at Cut 'N Curl chatting with the manicurist. The Sphinx asking a group of school children, "What did the mayonnaise say to the refrigerator?"

RE-ENTRY WOMEN

I was only a part-timer, so I was flattered when the department head asked me to teach this particular night class.

"You're young," he said, "but you're patient, and a lot of these gals haven't been inside a school of any kind for a long time. Take it easy on them. Keep your standards up, but take baby steps, all right? We want them to like college. We want this to be a good experience. Just keep your pants on."

I had a girlfriend, and I wasn't like that anyway. I didn't like trouble.

And neither, as things turned out, did any of my students. They were nervous at first. College, even a city college, was a big step for them. But they were, from that first night, cooperative and diligent. Their husbands or boyfriends were another story.

Did Mrs. G show her husband the journal where she'd written, "I am not taking no shit, no more, from nobody!" and did that explain the black eye?

And what about Nellie's boyfriend who found me in the men's room and hissed, "What you doin' with all that nookie, man?" I replied, "Tonight I taught the sentence fragment."

At mid-term, the class ran a little overtime and one of the men flung the door open and shouted, "What the fuck is goin' on in here!?" I told him we were finishing a difficult assignment and when he took a menacing step toward me, all my students rose as one. They brandished their pens, and he fled.

At the break they stayed in the room, did homework, and talked about what was on sale and where. They exchanged phone numbers and lied for each other. They told me that Sheila was coming back soon. And Kinisha couldn't get a babysitter, but she had all the assignments and was keeping up.

We started with thirty in January. By June, fifteen were left. After the final exam, they shook my hand or hugged me innocently. I'd become a kind of eunuch, somebody who opened a door and then stepped aside.

I went home that night, restless and melancholic. My girlfriend had moved on.

I opened a beer and turned on the Sci-Fi channel hoping for a moon man with Velcro holding his space suit together. Instead I got a fleet of battered rocket ships on their way home from Mars. Re-entering the Earth's atmosphere, they shook violently, and some who had taken the worst of it on their arduous journey couldn't bear up under the strain and flew apart.

RED RIDING HOOD TELLS HER MOTHER WHAT HAPPENED

Like, where to even start. So, okay—at the beginning. Right. So I've got the basket of goodies you gave me for Grams, and I'm remembering what you said about the forest, but now that I'm like safe, I can tell you I was totally looking forward to that part. With the wolf and all. I'm into danger, okay?

So I'm in the woods, and I hear footsteps, or like pawsteps, and it's him. And he talks. I'm thinking, "Nobody at school will believe this. Wait till Shaunelle hears!" So first he's all into "my pretty" this and that, like I haven't heard it all before. Anyhow, we chat, and he gives me his e-mail and some more insincere compliments, and the next time I see him he's in Gram's bed, and she's like inside him! Wait till I tell Amber that! I am so sick of hearing about how her grandma goes to Cabo all the time and paraglides and scubas. Those things are like nothing compared to being swallowed whole. And it kind of makes me want to know what that's like. So I let him.

It's weird inside a wolf, all hot and moist but no worse than flying coach to Newark, but it's not awful, and the wolf goes to sleep and snores so loud it's kind of funny, so Gram and I talk about when Dad lived with us and the noises that came out of him. Gross.

Then we hear footsteps and an argument, and then snip, snip, snip we're out! It's this cute woodsman. So, we're safe and really grateful, and I listened to a little lecture about Stranger Danger, which was weird because he's basically a stranger. Then we ate, and I kissed Grams good-bye, and the woodsman walked me to the edge of the forest where he said, "Maybe next time you'd like to see my axe." Which would make my English teacher like light up because she sees symbols everywhere, but to me it just sounded like a guy who didn't get out much and couldn't afford cable. So, is there pizza or something in the freezer because I am starved!

SEX WORLD

When I worked at the porn shop, sometimes my girlfriend Gwen would come with me and study. I was on a kind of perch, so I could watch for shoplifters. We must have made quite a picture—me on a tall stool beside the cash register, she at my elbow engrossed in a book.

Just her presence seemed to irritate some customers. One patron handed me a ten dollar bill and a copy of *Barely Legal*, but he directed his complaint at her. "You think you're quite the little judge and jury perched up there, don't you."

I knew what he meant. That smirk of hers spoke volumes—*I'm not prowling these aisles. I'm not skulking in those vespertine corners*. It irritated me that she'd irritated him. On my own, I kept a straight face, made change and said, "Thanks for coming in."

"You know," I told her, "Frank Sinatra said, 'Whatever gets you through the night.'"

She nuzzled me and replied, "That's the ticket. Cite the great philosophers. Now I'm hot."

Sometimes Gwen would put down a book like Sosa's epistemology text and help me stock the shelves. I thought she'd start in about empowerment and victimization. Instead we'd stare at some vista of skin and shake our heads in amazement. Who were these girls who seemed accident-prone? How else to explain the extreme poses they found themselves in if they hadn't been thrown from speeding cars?

At first, the job kindled our sex life. There were a few magazines with attractive people on well-made beds, and we pored over those. Gwen showed up more and more often at my room with her underpants already in her purse.

She liked it that my job was "interesting." She would whisper to her friends, "Ronnie works at Sex World." And they'd groan and want details, so I'd tell them about the customer who wore latex gloves as he riffled the glossy pages, or the dwarf who pretended to shoplift so I'd yell at him. Then her friends would pay for drinks, throwing twenties onto the table with abandon.

We might have broken up sooner if the picketers hadn't arrived, plainly dressed men and women with placards like GOD HATES FILTH and NO PORN IN OUR TOWN.

Gwen had ushered frightened girls through rabid demonstrators to get to abortion clinics, so she liked to walk beside me among the hectoring fundamentalists. I just wanted to keep my job because it was easy and paid fairly well.

Business got very slow. Not many of my regular customers were willing to walk that uncharitable gauntlet. But one did. Gwen and I both looked up when the door opened, and he came right to the elevated counter.

"I want to return this," he said. "On the box she looks like Marilyn Monroe. But not inside." He held up the pathetic, inflatable doll.

I just pointed to the sign that clearly said NO REFUNDS.

"It's not," he insisted, "anything like Marilyn Monroe."

Gwen chimed in, "Are you stupid? Can't you read? No refunds means no refunds."

Abruptly, he took a gun out of the pocket of his windbreaker. "For forty-nine ninety-five it's supposed to be almost real!"

Gwen had gone pale as skim milk. "Give him his money back, Ronnie."

"No," I said. "It'll come out of my check if I do."

The gunman turned toward Gwen. "Somebody has to. What about you?"

Gwen nodded, slowly picked up her purse and put it on the counter. She extracted her wallet, found a fifty dollar bill, and handed it over.

"Thank you," he said putting the deflated doll and the lurid box on the counter. "I'll give you the nickel next time."

As the door closed behind him, Gwen gasped, "You would have let that pervert shoot me."

"He wasn't going to shoot anybody," I told her. "I know that guy; he comes in all the time."

"Not with a gun! All you were worried about was your stupid fifty dollars."

"What do you know? Your daddy sends you a check every month."

"Is that how it is then?" she asked.

I couldn't look at her. "I don't know. I don't know anything."

Gwen put her thick book in her purse and climbed down. She had beautiful hair and perfect white feet she doted on, going to a salon every week where a Vietnamese refugee lavished attention on them and was tipped handsomely.

SOUTH

I was eleven the first time I went hunting with my dad and his brother. I sat in the back with the dog. He was excited and slobbered. We only went maybe four hours away from home. We left my mom and her sister and school behind and started off in the dark with the guns and the dog and the food and the booze and the boxes and boxes of twenty-gauge shells. Dad and my uncle seemed different. Amped. Bitching about Mom and my aunt and how they cooked the same crap all the time and didn't want to do you-know-what and talked on the phone night and day and spent money like it was water. I'd heard some of it before, but, man, nothing like this.

We get to the cabin and it's crummy. Like a shack with an outhouse. A big lake. Where the ducks are. Or soon will be. Dad and Uncle Mike start drinking. I've got a book, but they take that away. I start to text my friends, but they grab my phone. "Forget that crap." I try and play with the dog, but Dad tells me, "Leave him alone. He's got to work tomorrow." I just look out the door. There's other cabins. Smoke from their chimneys. I see another kid maybe a hundred yards away. He shrugs and I grin, but he probably can't see. Dinner is worse than anything I ever ate. I just go to bed.

Next morning, we get up early. It's dark. More drinking before we go to the blinds. It's cold. Other dogs bark. We hunker down. I see all the guns and think, "Go somewhere else, ducks." No way. They come gliding in, and all hell breaks loose. The dog gets busy. My ears are ringing. Everybody gets their limit pretty fast. I have to carry a couple. Dead ducks. Like the old saying. They're still kind of warm. Their eyes aren't even cloudy. Yet. That's when I get the feeling—I'm traveling, too. Not going south exactly, but traveling through my life. Like those ducks. And some make it and some don't.

SIRENS

From the ship's railing, Nikolos Vassilliadis watched the village of his youth emerge. First a ghostly blur, but soon a dazzling palette of white punctuated by colored awnings and umbrellas. Finally the shore with its terrible rocks, the ones that kept away all but the hardiest tourists.

Nikolos sighed. Why did he bother? He could have died in New York among his friends and former students, some of whom had gone on to great triumphs. In their interviews or memoirs, some spoke of working with "Saint Nikolos," standing in his small studio, the maestro's hand lightly on their throats. None of them knew he had to leave his homeland because his voice, his instrument, had disappeared almost overnight.

Nikolos was barely down the gangplank when someone addressed him, "Maestro."

"Christos! My old friend!" Very old. Still, they embraced.

"I have work for you," Christos said.

"Don't be absurd. I've come here to die."

"Before that. One last lesson. Don't decide now. Let's have a drink."

They walked away from the shops with their ZEUS ON THE LOOSE T-shirts and found a familiar taverna. On the way, they passed fishermen mending their nets and bragging. Nikolos knew many of them and remembered their cruelty and scorn. Their malevolent laughter.

"Look who's back," one of them shouted. "The braying donkey!"

So he and Christos had a drink. And then another.

Next morning he awoke in his old bedroom. The rest of the house was empty. Someone had cleaned out the spider webs and brought clean linen. His head hurt; why had he agreed to meet Christos and those children? He sliced bread and made coffee. As he ate he looked out the window at the rocks in the harbor. Huge and deadly.

"Nikolos!"

When he turned, there was Christos with three young women. Not children exactly. Girls. Pretty but peculiar. Shy, painfully shy.

"Raised by nuns," Christos said sounding like a pimp.

"I'm sorry, my friend," he said. "I've changed my mind."

"Just one minute of your precious time. It was a climb to get here. It wasn't easy for them." Christos pointed to where their feet would be if he could see them under the heavy shifts they all wore. "But water first, please," Christos asked. "It's very hot."

Nikolos shrugged as Christos brought the pitcher to his charges, who drank greedily. They seemed to delight in spilling cupfuls on their clothes.

"Now girls," said Christos. "Sing for the maestro."

Nikolos slumped in his chair. Teaching children.

Then, never lifting their eyes from the floor, they sang. Nikolos thought he was having an attack of the heart. What he was hearing was beautiful. More than beautiful. Sublime. Magnificent and sublime. He couldn't help but stand weeping. He struggled toward them. To be closer. To hear better, to have that music invade his body.

Christos stopped them. "See?" he said. "Imagine what they'll be like with a little refinement. Which you can provide."

"How did you find them? Where did they come from?"

"They're my neighbors' great-grandchildren. Their family has been on these islands forever and a day. All the women in their family can sing. So you'll teach them, yes?"

"Of course, yes." He looked out the window at the fishing boats. "They've given me a reason for living."

They didn't need much. Adjustments, mostly. And they learned fast. He could only work with them phrase by phrase. Any more than that made him feverish and crazy.

It was a week or two later that he approached the owner of Athena's Hideaway, a restaurant and bar closest to the harbor. The girls stood by the wall, drinking glass after glass of water as Nikolos negotiated. The owner was not so sure. He already had musicians.

Nikolos asked them to sing. Just a few bars. Immediately the deal was struck. They would bring in customers by the droves.

It was late afternoon. The local fishermen were on their way in after a long day when Nikolos led the three girls to the bandstand. Intrigued, a handful of tourists looked up from their grape leaves and beer. The girls were pretty, but awkward. They certainly weren't dancers.

Nikolos kissed each one on the cheek. He activated the sound system, adjusted the microphones, turned the huge speakers toward the ocean, and nodded for the girls to begin.

When they did, everyone stopped eating. They rose from their chairs, mesmerized, and stumbled toward the bandstand. Nikolos made their way among them, working his way to the edge of the patio and watching the small ships in the harbor suddenly raise their sails again. He could see by the wake and the lifted prows since those with engines had turned their throttles as high as they would go. The boats raced for shore, crushing those sailors who had leapt overboard in their rapture.

Even with his ears stuffed with wax, Nikolas imagined he could hear the cries of the stricken as the boats of his enemies broke against the rocks and disappeared.

SWEET & SAVORY

Norberto left his apartment in an agitated state and took a cab straight to the other side of the tracks. As he turned onto Night Street, he passed a blonde sitting in an open window beside a pie, and then a brunette holding a casserole. But he hardened his resolve and went straight to Chez Appetite. There he was informed he'd have to wait until Monique wasn't busy.

He settled on the couch, suddenly grumpy and out of sorts. It wasn't just that *Road & Track* and *Nugget* had replaced *Food and Wine*, and it wasn't just the terrible Maxwell House coffee. It was the reality of the situation. Upstairs, Monique could be serving duck roulade to some clodhopper.

It was painful to imagine her bidding the bumpkin good-bye, clearing the table hastily, and hiding the dirty dishes. How could she pretend that she had time to prepare the demi-glace!

Abruptly he stood up and left without a word. On the street he hesitated. To the left lay broad, lighted avenues with taxis like sedated alligators. To the right, more of Night Street with tawdrier though admittedly less expensive pleasures. Sordid, perhaps, but incandescent and abrupt.

Like that girl with the tattoo and soiled toque leaning on the smeared counter of Hotter Than Hot Donuts. Oh, those morsels of subtle shape and fragrance, succulent and lush.

She accepted his cash with a knowing smirk as Norberto, eyes closed, let that first bite linger on his tongue.

TELL ME A STORY

"Which one?"

"How you and Mommy met."

"You've heard it a hundred times."

"Please!"

"All right. Well, I needed a job."

"Because you were poor like an urchin in a fairy tale. And Grandma was sick."

"Who's telling this story? But, yes, I was broke and the only job I could find was dressing like a giant hot dog and standing on the corner in front of Mr. Weenie. But I applied for it, anyway.

"'Can you cavort?' asked the manager. 'You look nimble.' I was impressed by his choice of words."

"Because you'd been working for ignoramuses."

"Exactly. Now the costume—six-foot bun, five-foot wiener, tights—was easy to get into and warm without being too warm. Only my face showed, and not all of it.

"Turns out I was an ace cavorter. Business picked up almost immediately, and I got a small raise. Then one Friday a secretary with a name tag around her neck—"

"Cindy McAllister."

"Yes. Cindy McAllister invited me to a party. I thought, *Why not*. Mother was playing cards with other invalids.

"I took a bus to the party. I noticed how everyone's mood improved the minute I started down the aisle. Now they'd have a story to tell at dinner.

"Cindy's house turned out to be a duplex in a bad part of town. Motorcycles were parked in front of 11121½. Their riders leaned on them and smoked.

In civilian clothes I would never have talked to those thugs but my costume made me bold. I said, 'I'm looking for Cindy.'

"'Probably inside,' one of them snarled, 'making out with Colonel Mustard!'

"Then I knew he was in a costume, too. The leather pants and jacket. The open shirt. But he was a kid at heart. Playing *Clue*.

"Cindy was inside looking very different. A tattoo showed. Her shorts were threadbare on purpose. She said, 'Glad you could make it, Mr. Weenie.' She gave me a beer. I wandered from one small room to another. Many of the revelers were my former classmates from high school. No one recognized me. A girl from the homecoming court offered me a cigarette. I said, 'No thanks, I'm cool.' She said, 'You're supposed to be hot, Dawg, but let's boogie, anyway.'

"The way she danced embarrassed me. I think my large bun inspired her, but I was glad when the song was over. I enjoyed being incognito, and also I enjoyed the way people deferred to me. One guy looked at me by the snack table, sheepishly returned his cocktail frank and reached instead for a carrot stick.

"Eventually I found myself on the couch beside a plain girl in a modest dress. 'Friend of a friend,' she said before I could ask. 'I figure why not go to a party. All I do is work and take care of my dad who's sick.'

"I told her, 'My mother is ill.'

"'Small world.'

"She looked me up and down. 'You're getting paid to wear that. I hope.'

"I explained. 'I came from work.'

"'Me, too. Wanna dance?' she asked. 'I've seen you out in front of Mr. Weenie. You can bust some moves when you want to.'

"The song was a slow one, an old doo-wop version of 'In the Still of the Night.'

"I'd taught myself the box step by reading a book. When my partner knew I wasn't going to walk all over her feet, she relaxed. We exchanged names. Roz asked, 'Ever been rude to your body? Like telling your face that it's ugly?'

"'All the time.'

"'Well, I'm not doing that anymore. I spend fifteen minutes a day apologizing to parts of my body that I've denigrated. You should try it.'

"'Sounds like a good idea.'

"The next song was a disco number, so we sat down again. Her head fell against my shoulder and she dozed off. I sat very still. When she woke up, she looked at her watch. 'Walk me home, okay? I just live a couple of blocks from here.'

"Hand in hand we ambled by a vacant lot. People shouted at me from passing cars: 'Yo, Mr. Weenie!!' At the curb sat the burned out shell of a station wagon. Roz led me up the narrow walk of a pink house with bars on the windows. Inside she said, 'Daddy, I'm home!'

"An old man sat at a Formica table in the kitchen staring down at a checkerboard. 'Do you play?' he asked.

"I knew I was in a strata of society where nothing surprised anyone. Not ill health or bad luck or random gunshots or a stranger dressed like a hot dog.

"I played Roz's father while she counted out pills then watched while he swallowed them. After that she led me to the door.

"She said, 'I just wanted you to see what you were getting into.'

"'He beat me in seven, clever moves. He showed no mercy.'

"'Good answer,' she said. She kissed me, and we've been together ever since."

I adjusted my daughter's covers. "Goodnight, sweetheart."

"But it's not finished. Finish it!"

"A year later, you were born, okay? Now go to sleep."

TERRORIST

When the word came from the cockpit that the passenger in 22B was on the No Fly list, Steph, the flight attendant, took a deep breath and started down the aisle. Upon reaching the suspected terrorist, she smiled down at him, licked her lips and lowered herself onto his lap. Both arms went around his neck. Both legs flew up, the golden sheen of her calves picked up the overhead lights. Then she crossed her ankles demurely.

"What are you doing?" He muttered and squirmed.

"You are just cute enough to eat." She traced his jaw line with an index finger.

He hissed in her ear. "Stop! I have explosives."

"Really? Let me see if I can find them."

One hand dipped inside the terrorist's shirt. Perspiration broke out on his forehead as her fingers seemed to count every rib.

"All I feel," she said, "are your hard muscles and the kind of skin that, I admit, incapacitates me."

"They are in . . . ," he stuttered. "They are inside . . . they are deep in a body cavity."

She kissed one eyelid, then the other. "I love it," she whispered, "when you talk like that."

The terrorist whimpered. His hands crept to her shoulders, then to her face. He held her head like a melon, then closed his eyes and leaned in to kiss her.

That's when the co-pilot, who had been pretending to chat with a child in 16A, hit him with the butt of his pistol.

The flight attendant leapt from the terrorist's lap, screaming and brushing at her clothes as if they were covered with fire ants. The co-pilot battered the terrorist, tearing at his hands, raising them as high over his head as they could go.

"Nice work, Steph," he shouted. "That took guts."

But Steph was busy throwing up into an airsickness bag even as passengers crowded around, patted her on the back, and tried to shake her already shaking hands.

MOTIFS IN FOLKLORE & MYTHOLOGY

It's been a long book tour, and he's tired. The ceiling of every Holiday Inn looks the same. Even the ranks of pretty co-eds have thinned. Tonight this lecture hall is only half full. It's badly lit, too, and he can swear that something scuttled across his foot as he waited to be introduced.

Applause is scanty. There's a murmur, low and susurrus. Peckishly he waits for it to die down, gripping the lectern with both hands, only moving to brush back the lock of black hair that falls across his forehead in every photograph.

But the vague rustle and hiss don't diminish. He frowns and plunges ahead, rushing through the introduction about how folklore validates and transmits a culture's morals and values.

His listeners stir in the vast, crepuscular room. Now he can see that they're all women wearing shawls and long skirts. Unfortunately, not the fashionable kind with a cleverly placed slit so an expensive boot can show its one punishing heel. And no one's holding a notebook and staring with clear, adoring eyes. They're looking at him askance.

"Tell us a story!" someone demands.

Others join in, "Yes. You're the folklorist. Tell us a story!"

He looks at his notes. Why not? One story, and then the mini-bar at the motel. He clears his throat: "A disagreeable widow has one disagreeable daughter and one who is sunny. And beautiful, of course. The latter meets a tattered woman at the well, gives her a drink of water, and is rewarded: every word from her lips will be accompanied by a flower or a gem.

"Hearing this and seeing a pile of diamonds and roses on the kitchen table, the older sister sets off for the well where she insults the same fairy. Her punishment? Vipers and toads piggyback on every noun and verb.

"The moral, I believe, is clear." With that he closes his leather-bound notes, smiles, and says, "Thank you for coming. Good—"

"You forgot the prince," someone croaked. "The handsome prince."

"There is," he said, "a variant of the story where the comely maid meets a prince in the forest."

"And he marries her."

"Of course."

"And what about the other sister. The disagreeable one. She dies, doesn't she."

"According to Grimm, yes."

"Come down."

He peers into the gloom. "Pardon me?"

"You're finished, aren't you?"

"Oh, you want me to sign a book. Of course."

He makes his way carefully down the three steps, retreating almost immediately when he treads on something soft and damp. Then he hops over that—he knows how that must look and regrets it—and makes his way to the foot of the stage. Where a crowd has gathered.

He takes out his Mont Blanc pen with a flourish. "Who's first?"

"Do you know even another version," a crone asks stepping up to him. Close to him. Very, very close to him.

"What other version? I don't believe—"

The crone says, "The older sister doesn't die but goes into the forest where it's always damp and cool. She becomes queen of the vipers and toads. Her subjects sit at the queen's feet in the moonless night. They look up and beg, 'Speak and speak again. Speak until the world is covered with your bounty.' And she does, opening that incredible mouth and telling them the story of revenge and retribution, every word of which runs under their clothes and makes them squirm with delight."

A high-pitched cackle pierces the heavy air. Serpents fall from every pair of lips and slither toward him. He screams and flees. Tries to flee. But the floor is slippery and capricious. Down he goes, hitting his head. He moans and as he does, a viper plunges into his mouth going deeper than the tongue of the pretty sophomore who left his room in tears just forty-eight hours ago.

FLANNELGRAPH LESSON

We sat in very small chairs in the basement of the First Baptist Church. Mr. Powell was our Sunday School teacher. Using an old flannelgraph board, he told us stories from the New Testament, moving the one-dimensional donkey toward Jerusalem with Jesus essentially standing on its back like a trick rider. Every now and then one of the saints would plummet from the blue background. A glance from Mr. Powell kept us quiet as he calmly retrieved the disciple and put him in the upper right-hand corner in a kind of corral with Mary and Martha, a few camels, a tree, and a serpent.

He was always stepping out of the room. Who knew what his reasons were. Adults were a complete mystery to me and my friends. When we were alone one of us—we were separate from the girls—would go up to the board and do something silly. We were five or six years old, too young to be truly hateful or mean. We'd just make the serpent bite Mark on the butt or we'd race the camels until they fell off the edge into a void. Then we'd put everything back.

One Sunday, I made the Virgin Mary lie down and had a sheep kiss her on the lips. It was hilarious, and though we could almost stop laughing when we heard Mr. Powell returning, there wasn't time to undo what I'd created.

He looked at us, red-faced from choking back laughter. He glanced at the flannelgraph. We stopped giggling and concentrated on our polished shoes. Finally he said, "Looks like Mary really liked that little lamb." Then he grinned, and we erupted with—I'm choosing my words carefully here—joy.

A few weeks later, Mr. Powell's wife was killed down on the beltline by a drunk driver. The Sunday after the funeral he came to church looking ashen. Pushing aside offers from parishioners to take him home or to rest in the parsonage, he went downstairs and we followed.

When we were seated in the usual semicircle, he looked at us blindly before, one by one, he took the figures off the blue background. First he tore the fluffy cloud in two, then all the animals. As we watched open-mouthed and barely breathing, he tore the heads off the disciples. Then he reached for Jesus.

One of us squeaked, "Don't!" But he did it anyway. The headless body had barely reached the floor when we threw ourselves at him before he could get his hands on God.

THE GARDENER'S FUNERAL

There were some real barrio moguls: shaved heads, prison tatts. But behaving themselves. "Housebroken cobras," as Lorca liked to say. The animals that are our bodies prowled for a while, then I stood under power lines beside a girl with a bleeding heart and a lacy bra. The trees were close but looked far away and painted on the sky.

Santiago's body was elsewhere in a suit, probably with a handkerchief over his face. When it was my turn with the widow, I pronounced the hard consonants of my name. "Ah, sí," she said. "I remember. Santiago said you have the most beautiful bougainvillea."

I ate everything anyone handed me, then said good night a hundred times. Past the kids with a soccer ball, past the babies saying their secret names, across Rooster Comb Bridge, all the way to my beautiful bougainvillea that will soon need pruning.

THE PERFECT CRIME

Megan looks through Ben's briefcase for a felt-tip pen and, among the loan documents and an agenda for a meeting of state-wide realtors, she finds a separate sheet titled THE PERFECT CRIME.

Barely breathing, she reads the first few items:

In a park or mall where there's lots of other DNA

In another town

In the early hours of the morning

Thick gloves, common brands

In a panic, she calls her friend, Tawny, someone Megan has always admired because she actually is tawny—golden-skinned, jungle-scented, with a way of padding around a cocktail party as if she were barefoot.

"Oh, pooh," says Tawny. "They all find that on the Internet sometime. How long have you guys been married?"

"Fourteen years."

"That's about right. Remember when Ben had his affair? Who was it, that slut who worked at the Dairy Queen?"

"Children's librarian."

"That's right. What is it with men and that Mother Goose outfit? Anyhow, that was the seven-year itch. This is the fourteen-year itch."

"He wants to kill me!"

"Not really. He's just bored. Listen—go to the hardware store sometime this week and get a cheap pair of thick gloves, any old brand. While he's in the shower, put them on the dresser by his wallet where he can't help but see them. When he says, 'What are these doing here?' You say, 'I was thinking we might have a picnic in the park sometime. By moonlight. Maybe over in Shelbyville.'"

"And then what happens?"

"The sex gets better."

"Are you serious?"

"Absolutely. Couple of times a week for sure. More if you invest in some skimpy underwear."

"So that's it?"

"For now. Call me in seven years. I know what you have to do then, but I can't tell you over the phone. Bye, Hon."

TWINS

We never argued about who was oldest by a minute or any of that nonsense. We never fought. Totally simpatico. I could see through her eyes; she could see through mine. Even in different rooms. We didn't need idioglossia. We just looked at each other, and we knew. We were nice to our parents because we needed them for a while. Then we'd leave. Our plan was to live together forever. In grade school we were charming because it was necessary. In high school, we'd wear slightly different things, then go into the bathroom, change, and I'd be her, and she'd be me. Any boyfriend was our boyfriend. They didn't have a clue. Then one day, she said Death was a bird pecking at her heart. I said that I felt it too. We took turns declining. I'd languish, she'd go to school. Then she'd languish, and I'd go. The doctors were baffled. When I was in the hospital, she'd kiss some boy and I'd get flushed and set the monitors off. I melted away except for the little boat of the soul. Our soul. It bobbed merrily. If you asked how she feels without me, I'd say she is not without me. We write and win prizes. There's her picture in the paper and behind her that smeared face in the window is me.

UNDERSTANDING FICTION

There was no such thing as an answering machine when I was a kid. So I would come in from playing basketball or working on the yearbook, and my mother would meet me at the door. So-and-so had called and wanted to talk to me.

But she never said "wanted to talk to me." She used more vivid and forceful language. Someone was "dying to talk to me" or "couldn't wait to talk to me."

I knew the call was probably about homework or some harmless gossip, but I said, "Wow. Okay. I'd better get right back to them!"

Later, at dinner usually, she would ask me if everything was all right. I'd reply that I'd taken care of things, but it hadn't been easy. I'd been able to act quickly thanks to her. Then I'd help with the dishes. After that, she and my father would sit in the living room while he drew plans for a rocket car, sleek and dangerous, with a single seat and a long needle-nose.

I knew she was unhappy and was just glad that she didn't drink or run around with men. Some of my friends' mothers did that, and it was awful.

One day I came home from school, and Mother was on the phone. She pressed the receiver to her breast so the caller couldn't hear. "You'd better take this," she said. "Mona sounds desperate."

The phone was hot and moist when I took it, and I said, "Mona, what's wrong!"

"Nothing. Want to meet down at the lake?"

"I'll be right there!" Then I turned to my mother. "If I'm not back by seven, call the police!"

Mona was waiting when I ambled to the end of the dock. Her parents were alcoholics. My friends and I took turns essentially babysitting her. She'd rather be anywhere but home. She was also prim and religious, not wild like the daughters of other alcoholics. Spending time with her was just a good deed. She and I sat and watched the sun go down. After an hour or so she said, "They're passed out by now. I'd better get on back there and make sure the house isn't on fire."

When I got home, Mother was waiting on the porch. I told her that Mona and I had argued. She felt betrayed by the attention I'd been paying to Charlotte, who was sexy and vivacious. When I didn't deny anything, Mona drew a knife, and we struggled.

"Oh, my God." Mother clutched at her faded housedress. "And then what happened?"

GRAND AVENUE

My wife and I were jogging, like we do every morning. Down Mission, left at Trader Joe's, then up Grand Avenue and past the stately houses we will never be able to afford. We'd just turned the corner by Señor Fish, scattering a flock of pigeons strutting their stuff. One of them took off late, veered right into the path of a silver Lexus, then lay against the curb beating his one good wing like he was trying to put out a fire. My wife asked me to, for God's sake, do something, so I turned the delicate head clockwise until I heard a click. Then darkness poured out of the small safe of his body. That is when I realized I used to merely love my wife. Now I would kill for her.

UNIVERSITY OF THE DARK

George woke up in a building. An enormous building. Huge and imposing. Books from the floor to the ceiling. Thousands and thousands of books. Millions, maybe. Framed by computers stood a tall woman. Middle-aged. Glasses on a chain. Utterly composed.

"Am I glad to see you!" George said.

"How can I help you?" she asked in a practiced whisper.

"You can tell me where I am."

"In the university library," she answered.

"What university is that?"

"The University of the Dark. Look around you. Why not take advantage of this unique opportunity." She pointed to a comfortable-looking chair. "What would you like to see first?"

George decided to humor her. He needed time to think. There were other patrons scattered throughout the huge room, all of them bent diligently over their books. "What do you suggest?" he asked.

"Well, *Time* magazine listed *The Great Gatsby* among the greatest novels ever written. Let's start with that."

A book appeared in her hand, and he took it. As he sat down, he thought, *There's a way out of every fix*. But because the librarian was watching him, he put that thought aside and opened the book.

It was wonderful! Nick Carraway was a pussy, but George liked Tom Buchannan and he knew twenty guys like Meyer Wolfsheim. And the broads—both good-looking and sneaky. Just the way he liked them.

He closed the book with a satisfied grunt as a red-haired woman trudged past him on her way to the desk. Back in the day, he would've made a move. Now he just watched as she conferred with the librarian, received a book, and carried it back to her table, adding it to the huge stack in front of her.

George rose and stretched. Under the librarian's watchful eye he strolled past the checkout desk toward two tall doors. He reached for the wide, brass bar.

"Ouch! Son-of-a-bitch!"

A chorus of "Shhhhh" made him turn. Everyone was staring.

He muttered, "Sorry," as he made his way to the librarian. He showed her his palm. "I burned myself."

"You don't want to go outside," she said. A book appeared in her hand "Here. This should appeal to you."

He took it and stared at the title. "*The Sun Also Rises*. You call that news?"

"Hemingway should suit you to a T."

George went back to his seat. There had to be another door. After all, everybody here had to come from somewhere, right? That's when he noticed the neatly lettered sign on the main desk:

11–5
Monday–Sunday

Fine. He'd wait until five.

George gave himself to the book. Jesus—Jake had his balls shot off in the war! But what a stand-up guy. The bullfights, the fishing, the parties. And the way that Lady Brett Ashley went off with the boxer and then told Jake about it. What a bitch.

Just then he heard a discreet chime. Everyone looked up from their books. Some stood, stretched, yawned.

Here we go, George thought as he got to his feet.

But nobody moved. In fact, they just settled back into the same chairs, glancing around wearily. The librarian put a few things away, locked a drawer, and sat down again.

George hurried to the desk. "What's going on?"

"I don't know what you mean."

"It's five o'clock, right? Time for cocktails. What are we hanging around here for?"

The lights dimmed. Everyone was looking up and wearing expressions of mute resignation.

"I'd return to your seat if I were you," said the librarian. "It'll be dark soon. The darkest dark you can imagine."

"I don't get it, lady. We sit around and read until the lights go out. Then what?"

"They come back on again in the morning."

"And then what?"

"We read."

"Every day?"

"For eternity."

George had taken a few punches in his day, but none rocked him back on his heels like those two words.

"Oh, God," George moaned.

"A little late for that," she said.

"But I'm dead. Isn't that enough?"

"Oh, there are a lot worse things than being dead," she whispered as darkness like ink poured over her, over George, over everybody.

WAITING FOR WOOD

Justin had read the script. Today he was Maximus Peenius, a depraved Roman emperor. Except for the cheesy costumes, it was business as usual: him, three girls, and Ice Rink, the part-time rapper.

Rob, the director, was a pain in the ass but he'd also given Justin a career. First as Sam Spunk, Detective, and then as Peter Eton, Fellatio Fanatic. And the girls, all high school dropouts from Arkansas and Minnesota with cut-rate boob jobs, were good sports. He hated to make everybody wait for wood. When that happened, they just sat around, smoked, and ate Cheetos. Which made things harder. Well, not harder, but more difficult.

"So, Justin," said Rob. "Get behind the red curtain and when I tell you to, come out with your scepter in your hand. Ice'll do Amber. Give him a minute or two, then get in on that. Order everybody around like the cruel ruler you are. Then some double penetration—you and Ice work that out—and finally the money shot with Angel and Raven, okay?"

Oh, man. Easier said than done. Viagra might help, but it made Justin sweat and turn red all over. Rob pointed out that they weren't making *Lobster Man & the Seafood Sirens*, so just find another way.

He parted the curtain. The girls were kissing and giggling in the jacuzzi. That used to be all he needed, but not lately. So Justin closed his eyes—

He imagined parking a blue, dented Sentra and walking toward a little house in Palmdale. He skirted a Big Wheel right beside the front steps and shook his head ruefully at the bare spots on the lawn. Inside, the kids didn't look up from the TV where a dog on a pogo stick shot into the stratosphere.

Rob yelled, "Justin? You ready?"

"In a minute!"

Wearing grey, baggy sweats and bunny slippers, his wife stood in the kitchen stirring something in a flame-scorched skillet. A box of Hamburger Helper lay on the counter.

"Hey," he said putting his lunch bucket on the messy table.

"Hey, yourself," she replied. "The dryer's broke again."

Blood surged under his toga.

"Rob!" he shouted. "Good to go!"

"Excellent! Quiet on the set. Action."

And the emperor stepped through the curtain.

MYSTERY TRAIN

Even before the train left the station, the party started, winding up and down the aisles, spilling into compartments and bathrooms, then flowing out again, led by giddy men in party hats and tipsy women throwing those thin, colorful streamers usually associated with New Year's Eve. Everyone held a cocktail glass, and champagne splashed harmlessly across bejeweled fingers. The laughter, though a bit forced, was infectious. An otherwise modest woman might put aside the wicker basket she had packed to economize and drink straight from the bottle of Mumms, while her husband found himself in the arms of a divorcee with smeared lipstick and a grimly determined demeanor.

But then there was the conductor—dark and thin and dour. He passed through the cars bringing with him a kind of stasis. Laughter died away, iPods were turned down, those who were standing, sat, those on their phones clicked Off.

Yet when the conductor entered and pointed to a sick, old man slumped against the window and breathing with his mouth open, there was a kind of rightness to it. A symmetry, in a way. What was his quality of life? And when that old-timer was gone—which was sad, granted, but he'd lived a full life—there was more room which might be taken up by somebody interesting and attractive.

What was not so symmetrical or right was when the conductor pointed to a passenger sitting quietly and reading a book. A husband and father with perfect blood pressure and no history of cancer or diabetes. Or even one of the bellicose businessmen, who even as he was led away, shouted into his phone.

And the thing no one could believe, much less understand, was that moment when the conductor chose a child, plucking it from its mother's arms, carrying it away as she entreated her husband to do something about the inevitable open door, the iron wheels, the wind, the high-pitched scream.

Such a pall fell over the travelers then. People wept, whereas previously they had only cried. They stared out the window as the train hurtled on. How could such a thing happen? What kind of world was this, anyway?

How could the sky be so beautiful with those two intersecting contrails left by the Blue Angels, that crack aerobatic team out of Pensacola, Florida. Everyone stared. So achingly gorgeous. Wicker baskets opened. A cell phone played a carefree tune. Drinks appeared, this time adorned with little umbrellas, which were seized immediately by ravenous fingers and hands.

BIOGRAPHICAL NOTE

Ron Koertge teaches at Hamline University in their low-residency MFA program for Children's Writing. A prolific writer, he has published widely in such seminal magazines as *Kayak* and *Poetry Now*. Sumac Press issued *The Father Poems* in 1973, which was followed by many more books of poetry including *Fever* (Red Hen Press, 2007), *Indigo* (Red Hen Press, 2009), *Lies, Knives, and Girls in Red Dresses* (Candlewick Press, 2012), and *The Ogre's Wife* (Red Hen Press, 2013). He is a contributor to many anthologies, such as Billy Collins's *Poetry 180* and Kirby & Hamby's *Seriously Funny*. Koertge also writes fiction for teenagers, including many novels and novels-in-verse: *The Brimstone Journals*, *Stoner & Spaz*, *Strays*, *Shakespeare Bats Cleanup*, *Shakespeare Makes the Playoffs*, and *Coaltown Jesus*. All were honored by the American Library Association, and two received PEN awards. He is the recipient of grants from the NEA and the California Arts Council and has poems in two volumes of *Best American Poetry*. He lives in South Pasadena, California, where he is seriously funny.